Other Series by Harper Lin

The Patisserie Mysteries

The Emma Wild Holiday Mysteries

The Wonder Cats Mysteries

www.HarperLin.com

Tea, Tiramisu, and Tough Guys

A Cape Bay Café Mystery Book 2

Harper Lin

Contents

Chapter One

I was bent over a cappuccino, carefully moving my milk pitcher to etch a design into the foam, when Mrs. D'Angelo burst into the café.

Making the perfect cup of tea at my café was a completely new challenge for me. I studied the information about temperatures and steeping methods on the laptop in front of me, but it was contradictory and frustrating. I wanted straightforward, black-and-white information, and that was anything but.

Coffee was an art, too, but it had always come easily to me because it was in my blood. Tea was foreign, not something Italians were known for.

Why was I researching tea? The week before, a lovely older British couple had come into the café and ordered a "cuppa tea" for each of them.

"We've heard such good things about this place!" the woman exclaimed as I made their drinks.

"Really? From whom?" I asked with a smile. I wanted to thank the kind local-business owner and be sure to mention the source to my own customers. We Cape Bayers all made it a point to recommend each other's businesses to tourists. The more great places people found in town, the more likely they were to come back, and the better off our little town was.

"Oh, everyone!" she gushed, her light-blue eyes sparkling.

I got the feeling she was a very enthusiastic person in general.

"Everyone says you just have the best drinks and baked goods on the coast!" She leaned across the counter and lowered her voice conspiratorially. "I know you specialize in coffee, but I'm sure you make a wonderful cup of tea as well."

I certainly hoped so. I'd spent the better part of my thirty-four years perfecting my coffee-making technique, having started as soon as I was tall enough to see over the counter while standing on a stool. I had never really contemplated tea-making technique, always just pouring hot water from the espresso machine over a tea bag and handing the whole thing to the customer. I wasn't sure whether or not that constituted a wonderful cup of tea.

"If you'd like to find a table, I'll bring your drinks around to you," I told her.

For the most part, I preferred to serve my customers at their tables. I feel that makes for a more personal experience. It's the same reason we use cups and saucers unless the customer specifically requests a to-go cup—to make the customer feel at home in our little café—at home, but with better coffee.

The woman and her husband sat down at one of the little tables along the exposed brick wall, and I brought their tea over to them. I set the cups down with a smile and walked back around the counter to watch them surreptitiously from behind the espresso machine. I know Brits are picky about their tea, so I wanted to see their reactions as they took their first sips. Antonia's Italian Café might have been known for our artisan cappuccinos and coffee drinks, but that doesn't mean I don't care about my customers' experience with other drinks.

I could tell they were trying to be polite, but they couldn't disguise the displeased looks on their faces as the tea touched their tongues. I waited until they each took another sip, in case my interpretation of their faces was wrong, but when they did raise the cups to their lips again, I saw the same look of dismay in their eyes. I had a feeling when they put the cups down that they wouldn't be picking them back up again.

I debated whether to go over and ask them about it or to stand my ground and see if they picked the cups back up. I ended up hesitating only a minute. I'm not the type to beat around the bush. I took a deep breath as I approached their table.

"Is the tea not good?" I asked.

The couple exchanged a look as the husband exhaled. The woman looked slightly embarrassed.

"Well, dear." She glanced at her husband again and sighed. "I'm sorry, it's not." She hesitated for a moment. "But we're British, and we're very particular about our tea. I'm sure it's perfectly fine for an American palate."

An American palate. I wasn't sure if that was an extremely politely phrased insult or just a statement of fact. Or perhaps the tea was really that bad, but she was trying to find something she could say that wasn't completely awful.

I stood for a moment, trying to figure out what to do or say. I would give them their money back, of course, but other than that, I wasn't sure.

"I'm so sorry," I said. The perfectionist in me kicked in. "What can I do to make it better?"

"Oh, dear, you needn't worry about it. Another drink will certainly suffice. What would you recommend?"

"Well, cappuccino—I know I make a good one of those—but it's important to me to learn how to make better tea. For the next time you come in," I finished with a smile.

The woman glanced at her husband again, and he gave a little nod. I was beginning to wonder if he ever spoke.

"It is more complicated than it seems at first glance, dear," she said hesitantly.

"If you're willing to teach me, I'm willing to learn."

"Pull up a chair and join us, then."

"Sammy, can you run the front for me for a few minutes?" I called into the café's back room as I pulled a chair over to the table where the Brits were sitting. The chair's style didn't match that of the table, but that was okay because none of the chairs did. The entire café was furnished with estate-sale and antique-store finds my grandmother had picked up when her namesake café first opened. Despite none of the furniture actually matching, it all came together to give the café a warm, cozy feel.

"Sure thing!" Sammy called from the back. Her blond head bobbed over the display case as she came around toward the front. The face of my trusty second-in-command was flushed from working over steaming-hot drinks in the middle of the steaming-hot summer. She flashed a brilliant smile at me and busied herself with wiping down the counter.

"By the way," I said, taking my seat at the table, "I'm Francesca Amaro. I own the café." That felt weird to say, but it was true. I'd inherited it outright when my mother passed away at the beginning of the summer.

"It's a pleasure to meet you, Francesca! I'm Rose Howard, and this is my husband Edward." She then started in on what she called the basics of good tea making. For the better part of an hour, she went over tea varieties, water temperatures, brands, and steeping procedures. After only a few minutes, I went to the back to grab a notepad and pen to take notes on all she was telling me. Good tea making was every bit as complicated as good coffee making, and I'd had no idea.

And that was what led me to research the intricacies of tea brewing, leaning on the front counter with the laptop set up in front of me, a tea-aficionado message board pulled up on the screen, trying to make sense of the conflicting information in front of me.

Earl Grey tea should never be brewed above two hundred degrees!

Earl Grey tea should never be brewed a degree below a full boil!

Steep for at least three minutes!

Steep exactly two and a half minutes!

This all made my brain hurt. But I was determined to become as good at making tea as I was at making coffee.

Rose Howard had coached me through the rest of her vacation, declaring the last cup I served her before she left town "perfectly acceptable." Comparing that to "perfectly fine for an *American palate*," I thought that was an acceptable outcome, for less than a week of practice. But I wanted to see my customers' eyes widen with pleasure when they tasted my tea, the way they did when they tasted my coffee. I was also determined to learn to create pretty pictures in my tea cups the way I could with a latte, but taste came first. Pretty could come later.

"How's it going?" Sammy asked, emerging from the back room, where she'd been sorting through our newest supply delivery and coming up behind me to peep over my shoulder at the screen. She had been keeping close tabs on my quest to conquer the world of tea.

"Oh, it's so confusing!" I groaned. I turned my head toward the ceiling and rubbed my eyes with the heels of my hands. Sammy chuckled as she patted me on the back.

"Coffee would be just as confusing if you hadn't been learning it since you were a baby."

"I don't know about that," I replied.

Sammy chuckled again. "Oh, trust me. When I started working here with your mom, I could barely understand instant coffee. Coffee is plenty confusing. Do you know how long it took me to understand the difference between a café au lait and a caffè latte? They're both coffee and milk! Their names both *mean* coffee and milk!"

"You know the difference now, don't you?" I asked, momentarily concerned.

"A latte's the one with regular coffee and milk, and the café au lait's the one with espresso."

I think my heart actually stopped for a second at hearing her get them exactly wrong. Had she been serving customers the wrong drinks the whole time? I spun and looked at her, only to be greeted by a wide smile and a twinkle in her blue eyes.

"Oh, you know I'm kidding!" she laughed.

I eyed her suspiciously.

"Latte is espresso, café au lait is coffee. You don't think someone would have complained in all this time if I was doing them wrong? You think your *mother* would have let me get away with that?" She reached out and gave me a big hug. "Franny, you know me better than that!"

She was right, as usual. I'd only been working with her since moving back to town after my mother's death, but I'd known her for years as she worked with my mother. She was always trustworthy and reliable and right about anything that mattered. There was no way she didn't know the difference between a latte and an au lait. Still, she'd nearly given me a heart attack there for a minute.

"Yeah, I guess I do. I just get a little touchy about the café."

Sammy laughed her melodic laugh. "I can tell!" She patted me on the back and went back to work, arranging the contents of our delivery.

"Did my tea come in?" I called back to her, remembering that my order of an assortment of high-end loose teas was due any day.

"I haven't seen it yet," she called back, "but I have a couple more boxes to go. I'll let you know if I see it."

I sighed, blowing a loose strand of my black hair out of my face. I was really anxious to get the new tea varieties and start playing with them, but I resigned myself to the fact that I might just have to wait another day.

"What are you huffing and puffing about?" I heard a teasing voice ask in conjunction with the ringing of the bell over the door.

I looked up to see Matt Cardosi, my longtime friend and neighbor and maybe soon-to-be boyfriend, walking into the café.

"Matty!" I exclaimed, reverting to my childhood nickname for him, something I did a little too often in public. I hurried around the counter to give him a hug.

"Hi, Matt," Sammy called from the back room.

"Hey, Sammy," he replied.

"What are you doing here?" I asked. Matt worked a couple towns over, so we didn't often see him at the café in the middle of the day.

He shrugged. "I needed to run by the barbershop and check on some things, so I thought I'd take the afternoon off."

Matt had inherited ownership of the town barbershop after his father was murdered a few weeks earlier, and he was still trying to get it all under control. He glanced around the room. "Flowers haven't died yet, huh?" he said, his eyes settling on a bouquet of roses in a vase on the counter.

"Nope," I replied, stepping over to stroke one of the blossoms. "It's impressive." The flowers had been delivered a week and a half earlier and were only then starting to show signs of wilting. I needed to make a note of the florist who delivered them so I could be sure to always order from them. Maybe I could start having fresh flower arrangements in the café. I would have to make sure whatever I used didn't have a strong scent that interfered with the coffee, though.

"Did you ever figure out who they were from?" Sammy asked, coming out of the back room, carrying a box.

"Nope. Just 'your secret admirer.'" I plucked the note from where it nestled among the roses and read it over again.

To Francesca. The beauty of these roses pales in comparison to yours. Signed, Your Secret Admirer.

I had assumed they were from Matt when they first arrived since we'd had a bit of a flirtation going on over the past few weeks, but he'd denied it at the time and seemed a little curmudgeonly about them ever since.

Aside from Matt, the only person I could think might have sent them was Chris Tompson, the sleazeball who ran a little cell-phone shop in town. I'd had some brief dealings with him a few weeks before, ending with him offering to take me out and show me around town. I'd turned him down, but I wouldn't have put it past him to keep trying.

The possibility that they could have been from a customer had also crossed my mind. No one took credit for them, though a smattering of customers complimented them. I'd kept on the lookout for anyone who seemed overly interested in them, to get a clue as to who my admirer was, but no one seemed like a contender. I wasn't sure if I liked the idea that I had a secret admirer or thought it was a bit creepy. In any case, the flowers were pretty.

"Well, here's something to keep you busy until you figure it out," Sammy said, closing the distance between us and hefting the large box into my arms. The top was partially open where she'd checked the contents, and the unmistakable aroma of tea wafted out.

"My teas!" I exclaimed, as excited as a kid on Christmas. Matt and Sammy chuckled.

"Well, now I know what to get you for your birthday," Matt said.

I maneuvered the box onto the counter and began pulling boxes and jars and tins of tea out of it.

"How much did you order?" Matt asked, surprised.

"Just a little," I replied.

"That's just a little, huh?"

I nodded. It wasn't just a little. It was a lot. I'd gone a little overboard. But Mrs. Howard had emphasized how different brands and varieties of tea could vary dramatically in how they tasted and behaved when brewed. She gave me the names of her favorites, of course, but encouraged me to try an assortment to determine what I liked best. That was all the push I'd needed to order almost every option from our supplier's catalog.

"Fran's a little excited about this tea thing," Sammy stage-whispered to Matt.

"I see that."

"I can hear you!" I interjected.

They both laughed.

The bell over the door jingled again, and all three of us turned to see who it was.

Chapter Two

"Francesca!" Mrs. D'Angelo exclaimed, bursting into the café.

I held back a groan and caught Sammy suppressing a giggle as Mrs. D'Angelo surged past her. Mrs. D'Angelo was a lovely woman but exuberant, to say the least. About once a week, she came into the café like a whirling dervish, completely unconcerned with who was there and what they were doing, to share some usually inconsequential bit of news, primarily with me, for some reason.

Sammy had said Mrs. D'Angelo used to do the same thing to my mother, so maybe that was just something else I had inherited along with the café. Maybe she expected me to pass on the news to my customers as I served them.

"Oh, Francesca! Samantha! Matteo!" she cried. She dug the red-painted nails of one talon-like hand into my shoulder, turning me away from the counter and toward her. She hugged me briefly and forcefully, then turned and extended her free arm out toward Sammy and Matteo, motioning for them to come closer while keeping a tight grip on me. They each stepped toward us, but I noticed they were careful to stay out of the reach of Mrs. D'Angelo's grasping arms.

"Oh, my dears, have you heard the news?" she asked. "It's just awful, just—" She gasped as though overcome by whatever terrible thing she had to tell us. "Just awful!" In my experience, "just awful" to Mrs. D'Angelo wasn't much of a concern to the rest of us. So far, that summer, "just awful" had been a body board—later found propped up against a lifeguard stand—going missing from one of the beach rental houses, the daughter of someone I didn't know losing her job out of state, and some teenagers breaking into the local high school to fill the principal's office with balloons as a prank.

"What hap–?" Matt started to ask, not realizing that Mrs. D'Angelo didn't really allow much of an opportunity to get a word in during one of her proclamations.

"There's been a murder!"

All traces of amusement vanished from Sammy's face at the same time Matt went pale. Only a short time had passed since his father's murder. The culprit had been put in jail, thanks to my own personal investigation and Matt's help, but I hadn't expected another murder so soon, either. Then again, nobody ever really expects murder, especially not in a safe town such as ours.

None of us spoke for a moment as we tried to process Mrs. D'Angelo's news.

"Another one?" I finally managed to ask.

"Yes!" Mrs. D'Angelo's voice was breathy. "Can you believe it? In our dear Cape Bay! Two murders in as many months! Good heavens, what is this world coming to? Things weren't this way when I was a girl!" She pulled me into another hard, furious hug.

"W-what happened?" I stuttered.

"He was stabbed! Stabbed to death! Right in the chest! They found him this morning in the parking lot of Todd's gym. He was there all night! Can you believe it? It's so awful!"

For once, she was right about it being awful. I was curious, though, why she had just referred to the place as "Todd's gym". I didn't know this Todd that everyone else seemed to. I considered that I might need to work on getting out of the coffee shop a little more to reacquaint myself with the town after my long absence. There were too many people and businesses I wasn't familiar with after having spent most of the past fifteen years living out of town.

"Who was it?" Sammy asked softly, having finally found her voice.

"Little Joey Davis! Oh, his poor mother! Poor Denise! She must be just devastated! Devastated!"

Joey Davis, Joey Davis. I ran the name through my head, trying to determine if it was someone I knew. The name sounded vaguely familiar, as though it belonged to someone who may have been a few years behind me in school, but I couldn't be sure.

"What time is it?" Mrs. D'Angelo asked, finally letting go of my shoulder to glance at her watch.

I rubbed the place where her fingers had been, expecting a mark there the next day.

"I need to go. The Ladies' Auxiliary will want to take meals to little Joey's mother, and I'll need to coordinate that." She looked pointedly at me and Sammy, whose eyes were filling up with tears. "The two of you are welcome to participate if you can make the time. Just let me know!" And with that, she bustled back past Matt and out the door.

Matt sneezed, probably from the overwhelming cloud of heavy floral perfume lingering behind.

I immediately went to Sammy, whose tears were threatening to spill over, and wrapped her in my arms. She held on tightly for a few seconds before letting go.

"Thank you," she whispered, wiping at her eyes.

"Did you know Joey?" I asked.

"Joe," she corrected. "He hasn't gone by Joey since he was little. Mrs. D'Angelo probably just calls him that still because his dad's name is Joe, too." She took a deep breath. "I went to school with him. He was my age."

Sammy was twenty-seven, so it made sense that his name only sounded vaguely familiar to me. I didn't know him, but I could have seen him or his dad around town even if I didn't know who they were. Cape Bay wasn't so big that residents weren't at least passingly acquainted with each other.

"We weren't close or anything, but we'd chat when he came in," Sammy went on. "He'd been having a hard time lately. He lost his job, had to move in with his parents—"

The bell over the door jingled as a customer came in, clearly a tourist, based on his loud Hawaiian shirt and the camera draped prominently around his neck. I found it strange that people didn't know they were dressed like a stereotype.

"Can you take this one?" Sammy asked quietly. "I just need a minute."

"Of course, of course, go, go!" I waved her off toward the back room, and she hurried away. "Hi," I said brightly, turning to the customer. "I'll be right with you." I headed around the counter to the register, where I could punch in his drink. "Matt, can you—" I started, motioning toward the pile of teas littering the counter.

"I got it," he said and started to put everything back in the box.

"What can I get for you, sir?" I asked the customer.

"I've heard you make a pretty good latte," the man drawled in a southern accent.

"That I do," I said with a smile.

"Then I'd like one of those, please, ma'am."

I told him the price, and he paid for the drink.

"If you'd like to take a seat over there, I'll have that right out to you," I said, handing him his change.

The man walked over to one of the tables as I pulled the espresso for his drink. After all the time I'd spent studying tea that afternoon, doing something I was comfortable with felt good. When the espresso was ready and the milk fully steamed, I poured in my design—a beach scene, complete with palm tree—to suit my customer's vacation style. My grandparents had perfected our family's method of brewing coffee, but I had elevated the drinks with my artistic creations.

I took the drink out to the man's table and set it down, the design facing him.

"Well, look at that!" he exclaimed. "If that's not the prettiest cup of coffee I've ever been served. You don't mind if I take a picture of it, do you?" He gestured at the camera around his neck.

"Not at all," I replied. "Please let me know if it doesn't taste every bit as good as it looks. I'll be right over there." I gestured toward the armchair Matt had parked himself in after he finished boxing up my tea order.

"Will do. Thank you, ma'am."

"Thank *you*, sir."

I headed over to the armchair next to Matt. The customer's back was toward me, so I couldn't see his reaction when he put his camera away and took his first sip, but he didn't immediately turn around to find me, so I figured that was a positive indication regarding the coffee's taste.

"So," I said to get the conversation started.

"So," Matt parroted.

I wasn't quite sure where to take the conversation next. "You okay?" I asked.

Matt sighed. "Yeah, just..." He paused for a moment to collect his thoughts, then took a deep breath. "Yeah, I'm fine. I'll be fine."

"Did you know Joe?" While I had moved to New York City after college, Matt had come back home. He knew a lot more of what had gone on in town over the past several years than I did. I was slowly catching up, but there was still a lot I needed him to fill me in on.

He shrugged. "Not really. Not too well. We'd say hello, but we weren't buddies or anything."

I nodded.

"Like Sammy said, he was a good bit younger than you and me, so we didn't really run in the same crowd." He chuckled. "Well, from what I know of Joe, we wouldn't really have run in the same crowd if we were the same age."

I raised my eyebrows, silently asking him what crowd Joe ran with.

Another shrug. "You know, just—"

I looked at him. I didn't know.

He sighed. "Sammy would know better since she went to school with him, but I kind of remember him being a big-shot athlete in high school. Baseball, and I think he might have boxed, too. I'm not really sure. My dad was the one who kept up with all that."

That was it? Just that Joe was an athlete? Matt hadn't been athletic back in school, but I didn't think that was enough to warrant the "different crowd" comment.

"I didn't think you hated athletes that much," I said. "Weren't you friends with some of the guys on the hockey team?"

Matt shifted uncomfortably in his chair. He had more to say. I could tell.

"Well—" He exhaled sharply and lowered his voice even though I had only the one tourist sitting in the café. "He was supposed to have a full ride to college for baseball, but he got caught with drugs or something and lost the scholarship. Things kind of went downhill for him after that."

Then I understood. Matt had always been a pretty straight-and-narrow kind of guy. He wouldn't have hung around with a guy who was into drugs.

The tourist stood up and glanced around. I hopped up out of my chair.

"How was the latte?" I asked, moving toward him.

"Best I've had in a long while," he responded with a smile. He held up the cup and saucer that had held his drink. "Where can I put this?"

"You can just leave it on the table, or I can take it from you. You definitely don't have to bus your own table." I stepped closer to him, took the dishes from him, and placed them behind the counter.

"Well, thank you, ma'am." He glanced around the nearly empty café. "Things always this slow in here?"

"No," I exclaimed with a laugh. "You came in at the slowest time on the slowest day of the week! Give it a day or two, and we'll be packed. Every week, there's a couple of days before the new batch of tourists finds us. We're busy in the mornings and evenings, no matter what. It's just the midday that takes a hit."

"Well, I'll be back for another one of those lattes before I leave town even if I have to fight a crowd!"

"We'll look forward to seeing you," I replied with a smile.

He turned to go, and I took his dishes into the backroom to be washed. Sammy was still there, leaning against the desk.

"How are you doing?" I asked.

She took a deep shaky breath. "I'm okay. I'm just kind of shaken up. I'm not sure why. I guess—just—you know…" She trailed off and took another deep breath.

"I know," I said. "If you want to go on home, it's fine with me. I'll be fine here alone, and if I'm not, I can call in one of the girls."

A couple high schoolers worked with us part time, in addition to a couple older women who helped out from time to time. At least one of them would almost definitely be available to come in and help me on short notice.

"No, I'll be okay." She stood up.

"Sammy?" I said, a warning tone in my voice. I knew she wouldn't want to leave me alone, but I also knew Joe's death was hitting her harder than she wanted to admit.

She sighed. "Are you sure?"

"I'm sure."

"Okay." She reached around her back and untied her apron, then pulled it over her head, her blond ponytail momentarily flipping up over her head. "Thanks, Fran," she said. She gave me a quick hug, grabbed her purse, and headed out the back door.

"I sent her home," I announced to Matt as I walked back into the main part of the café.

"That's probably good." He stood from his chair and stretched. "She looked kind of shaken up."

"Yeah, I figured it would be better for her." I leaned my hip against the counter. Even though I didn't know Joe Davis, Mrs. D'Angelo's announcement still bothered me. My entire life, Cape Bay had been a safe place, the kind of place where people barely locked their doors, especially during the off-season. We were a little more careful when tourists packed our streets. I found it troubling to think about having another murder in town. I was guessing it had at least doubled our usual murder rate.

"So where's this gym where Joe was found? And what's it called?" I asked Matt.

"Todd's gym? It's out on the edge of town. Near the marina."

I was happy to hear it was as far away as anything still in Cape Bay could be. "But what's it called?"

"Todd's gym," Matt repeated.

"I don't know who Todd is, and I don't care that it's the gym he goes to. I just want to know the name of it," I exclaimed, getting a little exasperated by how hard it was to get Matt to give me a straight answer.

"Franny"—he looked me in the eye—"the name of the gym is Todd's Gym. Todd owns it, and he named it after himself. And, yes, you do know him. It's Todd Caruthers."

Chapter Three

"Todd *Caruthers*?" I repeated.

Matt nodded. "You remember him, right?"

I certainly did remember him. Todd Caruthers had gone to school with Matt and me, graduating the same year we did. He was, in my eyes—and the eyes of most of the female population of our school—the be-all and end-all of high-school boys. He was tall, tan, and blond, with male-model-turned-movie-star good looks.

He was a three-sport varsity athlete, covering pretty much every variation of the all-American boy you could ask for—quarterback on the football team, star of the basketball team, and home run–hitting pitcher on the baseball team. He was the consummate athlete and the consummate jock, and I adored him. But there wasn't a chance a guy like that would give a shy, quiet girl like me the time of day. He was always dating one pretty cheerleader or another. Once in a while, he'd mix it up and go out with a girl on the field-hockey team, but the girls like me who were on the debate team and school newspaper never stood a chance. I pined away for him from a distance all through high school. So, yes, I remembered Todd Caruthers quite well.

I spared Matt my reminiscences of adolescent angst and limited my response to a simple, "Yes."

Matt could barely conceal his snort. "I bet you do."

Though he was looking down at the floor, I saw crinkles at the corners of his eyes. "What's that supposed to mean?" I exclaimed.

Matt shrugged and glanced up at me before quickly looking away again. "Just, uh, just that, well, I seem to recall you had a bit of a thing for him back in high school."

"What!" I screeched.

That made Matt laugh outright. "What? You thought it was a secret?"

I could feel blood rush to my face. "Yes, well, I mean, um—" I sputtered.

"Oh, come on, Franny! You went to every football, basketball, and baseball game he played in. *Even the away games.* You don't even like sports."

"I do so! I like the Red Sox and the Patriots!"

"That's because you're from Massachusetts. You practically have to swear on a Bible that you like the Pats and the Sox before they'll give you a driver's license," he joked. "I bet you can't even name the starting center fielder for the Sox this year."

I tried to think of every baseball player I'd ever heard of in hopes of getting incredibly lucky and blurting out the right name. *Babe Ruth? Joe DiMaggio? Mickey Mantle?* I was reasonably certain none of them had played in my lifetime, but I wouldn't bet on it.

Apparently my silence and wrinkled forehead were enough to convince Matt I had no idea.

"Yeah, I thought so," he said.

"I can't believe you knew." I hid my face in my hands.

"It's not like you were the only one. I think every girl got all drooly when he walked by. I never really thought anything of it." He shrugged.

I still felt embarrassed. As a teenager, I had put a lot of time and effort into making my interest in Todd or any other boy seem as inconsequential and nonchalant as possible. To hear, even fifteen years later, that it had been as plain as the nose on my face to everyone around me was completely mortifying—especially when the guy I was currently interested in was the one telling me.

"So," I said, deciding to move the conversation forward. "Todd owns a gym now?"

"Yup. Todd's Gym, like I said. The name's supposed to make it easy for you to know who owns it," he said with a smirk.

I gave him a dirty look in response. "What kind of gym is it? Like treadmills and weights or boxing or what?" When the tourist season died down, I would have some time to take an exercise class or two. I was hoping for some kind of yoga or spinning, but Cape Bay is a small town, and I knew my options might be limited.

"Lot of stuff. It's a big place. Two stories. Big concrete square." Matt gestured with his hands to indicate the large squareness of the building. "It's the only place in town, so I think he tried to cater to everyone."

"I might have to go check it out."

"Check it out or check *him* out?" Matt asked. I couldn't tell by his tone or his expression whether he was joking.

"The gym," I said out loud. I kept the rest to myself: *Jocks don't usually hold up over the years.*

Matt eyed me, looking somewhat suspicious, but really, what did it matter? Even if I was going over to check Todd out, he probably wouldn't even remember me. I had been completely inconsequential in his high-school experience. Besides, Matt and I had never discussed what was going on between us. A lot of dinners, a good bit of flirtation, and a few kisses on the cheek were as far as anything had gone. I was free to check out another man if I wanted to.

The bell over the door jingled, and a family of five walked in, all sunburned and sandy from their day on the beach.

Matt glanced over his shoulder at them. "You got this?" he asked.

I nodded. He was kind to check, even though I was pretty sure he couldn't figure out our espresso machine if his life depended on it.

"I'm going to go then," he said. "Let me know if you want to get dinner later, okay?"

"I have to go home and let Latte out. If you want to go out after that..."

"Sounds good. I'll see you." He rapped twice on the counter with his knuckles and waved before heading out the door.

"Hi, can I help you?" I asked, turning to the family of tourists. Out of the corner of my eye, I saw Matt hold the door open for another group headed into the café.

The rest of the day went pretty much like that—a steady stream of customers, one after the other—never more than I could handle on my own but always enough to keep me busily going from one task to the next, making drinks, cleaning them up, serving food, or wiping down tables. By the end of the evening, I was more than ready to turn the Open sign around to Closed.

I finished cleaning up, made sure the refrigerated display case was fully stocked with parfaits and fruit cups for the morning breakfast crowd, and headed toward home. The sun had already set, and night was quickly falling, so I walked out along the street instead of taking the shortcut through my neighbors' backyards. I probably would have stayed under the streetlights no matter what, just so I could see where I was going, but the thought of a murderer roaming the streets was lurking in the back of my mind, which kept me to the well-travelled route.

My house was just a few blocks away, tucked down a side street. It was a Cape Cod–style house surrounded by other Cape Cod–style houses. My grandparents had bought it shortly after their arrival in the country and raised both my mother and me there. Matt's house, the one he had grown up in and recently inherited from his father, was two doors down from mine. We were, by far, the two youngest people on the street.

As soon as I slid my key into the lock on the door, I heard canine feet running down the stairs. A wet nose poked out the door the second I cracked it open. It had only been a few hours since I'd last been home to let him out—he was equally excited to see me whether I'd been gone five minutes or five hours. I grinned as the dog jumped up on me in a desperate effort to cover my face with his kisses. I'd only had Latte a few weeks, but I already couldn't imagine my life without him.

He was a stray that I'd assumed was a mixed-breed mutt until I took him in to see the veterinarian.

The doctor's face broke into a grin when he walked in the door. "A Berger Picard!" he exclaimed in a French accent. "I haven't seen one of these since I came to the United States!" He immediately started ruffling Latte's fur as though he was a long-lost friend.

When I expressed my surprise at the vet calling Latte a purebred, he told me that the scrappy, scruffy appearance of the Berger Picard often led people to believe that they were mixed-breed dogs.

"But I can assure you, this dog is a Berger Picard," he said. "My family has raised these dogs for generations. After the world wars, we helped to rebuild the breed!" He gave me a meaningful look. "The wars were very hard on the breeders. It is difficult to feed your dogs when you can barely feed yourself."

He offered me a breed DNA test if I wanted to verify his assertion, but since Latte hadn't come with any papers, I didn't see the point in spending the hundred dollars on it. If my vet, an expert in Berger Picards, said that that's what Latte was, I would believe him. I loved the little guy no matter what his genetic background was.

I was happy to know a little more about him, though. He was sweet and friendly and affectionate, just like the breed description, which I later looked up, had said he would be. Even his perfectly latte-colored fur was typical of the breed.

I scratched behind Latte's ears with both hands. "Have you been a good boy? Are you ready for some din-din?" My voice had a more "baby-talk tone" than I would comfortably admit.

I went to the kitchen and scooped out Latte's dinner, then ran upstairs to my bedroom to change. I had a plan to clean all my grandparents' possessions out of the master bedroom on the first floor and redesign it for me to move into, but I'd only gotten as far as cleaning out the fifty years' worth of accumulated belongings. Someday soon, I needed to get to the hardware store to look at some paint colors and the housewares store to get some curtains and linens. I just hadn't had the opportunity–something else to add to my list for when the season ended.

I pulled off the black shirt and pants I'd worn to work–remnants of my New York City wardrobe–and pulled on a pair of jeans and a light-blue T-shirt that felt much more appropriate for a casual Cape Bay dinner. Glancing in the mirror, I smoothed my hair and ran a finger under each eye to clean up the little bit of mascara that had migrated off my lashes during the day. By the time I got downstairs, Latte was prancing at the door, ready for his evening walk.

I'd been enjoying the twice-daily walks he made me take. It felt good to get out and breathe the salt air as it blew in off the ocean. It wasn't as strong near my house as it was at the café, but I could feel it all the same. I felt as though I was home, safe and secure, the way I felt back when I was in high school and the world seemed like a much simpler place.

I didn't want to leave Latte home alone again so soon after getting home, so we stopped by Matt's house on our way. He answered the door, wearing jeans and an old T-shirt instead of the button-down and khakis he'd been wearing earlier. His dark hair was disheveled. I did think he looked pretty cute.

"You ready for dinner?" he asked. He noticed the dog standing by my side. "Latte coming with us?"

"That's actually what I wanted to ask. I feel bad leaving him home by himself. Would you want to go to Sandy's?" Sandy's Seafood Shack was the best place around for New England seafood, and since its namesake was the owner's former four-legged furry friend, they allowed dogs on the patio and would even bring them a bowl of water and complimentary snack. I'd never thought I'd be one of those people who take their dog out to eat with them, but well, there I was.

"Sure," Matt replied. "You ready to go?"

"Let me go get my purse, and I will be." I handed Latte's leash to Matt and jogged across the yard between Matt's house and mine. I unlocked the door, grabbed my purse from where I'd dropped it just inside, locked back up, and jogged back.

"You hungry or something? You were moving pretty quick there," Matt said with a laugh when I got back.

"Actually, I am!" I replied. The only thing I'd consumed since lunch was a single cappuccino, and it was nearly nine o'clock.

"Well then, let's go!"

Matt held Latte's leash as we walked toward Sandy's. One of the things I loved about living in a small town is that I could pretty much walk anywhere I needed to go. For the most part, the only time I got in the car was to go grocery shopping, and that happened only if I needed so much stuff I couldn't carry it all.

Sandy's wasn't busy. Another couple was eating inside, and a bunch of college kids were hanging around the bar. It was a pretty safe bet they were in town for summer jobs—lifeguards, waiters and waitresses, store clerks. A lot of businesses scaled up for the summer by hiring college students. I did find it strange while growing up that college kids wanted to come to sleepy Cape Bay to work for the summer, but I guess it's pretty appealing when you don't already live at the beach.

Matt and I stuffed ourselves on beer and lobster rolls while Latte munched on apples with peanut butter. When we couldn't eat any more, we headed back home. We went past his house to mine. Even when there weren't murderers on the prowl, he liked to walk me to my door. He claimed it was the gentlemanly thing to do, just like he claimed it was the gentlemanly thing to pay for my dinner almost every time we went out. I'd managed to sneak a few in here and there, but I thought it was a game for him to pay for both of our meals before I could object or pay myself.

We lingered at my door for a few minutes while I finished filling Matt in on my newest thoughts on tea preparation. I knew he wasn't exactly interested, but I appreciated him humoring me.

"And then I should be able to try to make tea-latte art," I said as I wrapped up my perhaps overly detailed explanation of how I was going to determine the perfect amount of milk to use in my tea drinks. In addition to my research into brewing techniques, I'd also been considering what tea-based drinks I wanted to add to the menu at Antonia's.

"Well, I'll be happy to serve as a taste tester for you when you need it," Matt replied.

I laughed and then yawned. "I'll keep that in mind. For now, I'd better worry about getting to bed."

Matt chuckled. "I'll see you tomorrow, then?"

"Yup, sounds good," I said, rocking on the balls of my feet.

"Okay." He handed me Latte's leash and started to let his hand fall back to his side, but he stopped and tucked a loose strand of hair behind my ear instead.

I held my breath.

Matt pushed his hand into his pocket. "Good night, then."

"Good night," I replied.

Matt turned to head home. I sighed and went inside to sleep.

Chapter Four

I woke up in the morning with Todd Caruthers on my mind—nothing in particular, just vague thoughts about the murder, the gym, and Todd from back in high school. I checked the time on my bedside clock. I had plenty of time if I wanted to check out Todd's Gym before I headed in to the café—to see if they offered any classes I was interested in, of course. Seeing how well Todd had held up—or hadn't—would just be a side benefit.

After showering, I pulled on a T-shirt and shorts, seeing no sense in getting more dressed up when I'd just have to change into work clothes in a few hours. I fed Latte and then took him for a quick walk around the block. I would have taken him to the gym with me, but I doubted they let nonservice dogs in.

"I'll be back to play with you before work, okay?" I said, ruffling Latte's ears in my hands as I got ready to walk out the door. "You're a good boy! Yes, you are!" I had somehow become a dog person when I wasn't paying attention.

Todd's Gym was just far enough away that I debated actually getting in my car and driving over there, but the weather was perfect, so I decided to walk. I followed the road I lived on out to Main Street, which followed the beach. It was late enough in the morning that the tourists had already started to fill up the beach, so I stuck to the road. I could only see the ocean through occasional breaks in the businesses lining the beach, but I could hear it and smell it, and that was enough to make the walk pleasant.

After almost half an hour, I came upon a large concrete structure my grandmother would certainly have called a monstrosity. Emblazoned across the structure in giant yellow letters was TODD'S GYM in all caps. The name definitely couldn't have been easily missed.

I walked up to the heavy glass double doors and pulled one open and was greeted by a rush of air conditioning. Just the entryway by itself was huge. I could've done cartwheels if I wanted to. The floor below my feet was a shiny black tile, and the ceiling had to be at least twenty feet above me. From where I stood upon walking in, I could see the entrance to a basketball court on my right and a room full of exercise equipment on my left. Beyond the basketball court was a metal staircase leading up to the second floor. I couldn't be sure, but I thought I detected the scent of chlorine coming from somewhere in the building.

Directly in front of me was a large reception desk with a perky-looking blond girl sitting behind it. I guessed she was about nineteen years old. Her ponytail was as high as it could possibly have been without actually being on top of her head. She had a fairly deep tan that I couldn't quite pin down as being from the sun or a bottle. She was wearing layered hot-pink and black tank tops and, presumably, skin-tight yoga pants. All that, combined with her full face of makeup, made me feel as though I was woefully underdressed and a little bit old.

"Hi! Can I help you?" she chirped.

"Um, yeah, I was wondering what kind of classes you offer?" I was still looking around the massive space, not quite paying attention to the girl.

"That's great. We have some brochures right here. Is there a certain kind of class you're looking for?" She stood up and began pulling shiny sheets of paper from a plastic rack on the counter. "We have all the usuals, of course: Pilates, yoga, *hot yoga*"–she raised her eyebrows as she mentioned hot yoga, clearly suggesting that class was one of their most enticing–"spinning, aerobics, dance fitness... water aerobics if that's more your style."

I groaned internally at that perky, fit young woman thinking that water aerobics might be the most physical activity I could handle. I took the brochures and started glancing through them. Apparently, I would have plenty of options when I had the time. I was about to ask her about their membership plans when a man came out of the back and leaned over the counter to talk to Perky Girl.

"Karli, were there any calls for me while I was gone?" he asked.

"Just one." She picked up a slip of paper from the desk and handed it to him. "Oh, this woman was asking about our classes."

I looked up into a stunning pair of deep-blue eyes. Todd Caruthers. Despite my expectation that Todd, as a former high-school athlete, would have gotten soft and maybe developed a paunch, he was every bit as handsome as he had been back in high school, maybe even more so.

"Franny? Francesca!" he exclaimed, as Karli took a phone call.

I caught my breath. *He remembers me?*

"Todd." I smiled.

He stepped around the curve of the desk and put his arms around me. His chest was every bit as muscular as I had imagined it to be in high school. He released me and stepped back. "I was wondering when I'd see you." In a lower voice, he said, "Did you get my flowers? I wanted to come by the café to see if you liked them."

The flowers were from *Todd*? I was speechless. Why had Todd sent me flowers, and why on earth did he sign the card "your secret admirer"?

"I, um, yeah. Yes, I mean, yes, I did." I was so thrown that I could barely put a sentence together. "I didn't know they were from you."

He grinned, flashing shiny white teeth. "You didn't? I thought you'd seen me when I came in to Antonia's."

I thought back, trying to think of when I might have seen him or how I might have missed him. *How could I miss Todd coming into my café?*

"No—no, I didn't. I guess I've had a lot on my mind." That was the only reason I could think of that I hadn't noticed him. With my mother's death and Matt's father's death and my investigation into his murder and learning how to manage the café all over again, I probably couldn't have told you most of the people who came in, even the ones I'd known my whole life. Matt and Sammy were really the only people I'd managed to connect with, and circumstances had thrown me together with them more than I'd sought them out. I figured I should reach out to more of my friends when the busy season ended.

"Yeah, I can see that. Still, my feelings are a little hurt!" He reached out and swatted me playfully on the arm. "You don't even notice your old friend, Todd?" His eye twitched in a wink.

My old friend? That's not exactly how I would have described our relationship. I almost wondered if he'd confused me with someone else, but he used my name, so he must have remembered who I was.

"Why didn't you sign the card?" I asked, trying to get away from the awkward question of why I hadn't noticed him.

"Oh, well, I wanted to play it cool. You've had a lot going on, and I didn't want to make anything complicated. But I thought you might like some flowers. Every girl likes flowers, right?"

I smiled. "Flowers are always good. And the ones you sent were beautiful. And still alive, surprisingly."

He smiled, a gleaming, sparkling smile that made me weak in the knees. "Great. I'm glad you liked them." He lowered his voice again and leaned in toward me. "How are you doing? Since your mother...?"

I was surprised by his compassionate question. He'd been such an arrogant jock in high school and hadn't seemed all that much different so far in our conversation, but maybe there was more to him after all.

"It's been rough. But I'm doing okay. It was a lot of change all at once."

Todd nodded. "And Matt?"

I was even more shocked. He was interested enough to ask not only about me but about Matt also? He really must have changed.

"He's getting there. Both of our parents' deaths were sudden, but emotionally, I think they were very different. An aneurysm, like my mother had, is so different from murder."

Todd nodded thoughtfully, but I realized with a sinking feeling what I'd said. I had mentioned murder when there had just been one in Todd's parking lot.

"I bet," he said sympathetically. He shook his head. "You know, I just keep thinking about Joe's parents—how they must be feeling right now. Did you know Joe? Did you hear—?"

I nodded. "Yes. Well, yes, I heard, but no, I didn't know him. Was he a friend of yours?"

Todd glanced around, checking on what Karli was up to at the desk, then took my elbow again and led me toward a door that led off the main lobby. I hesitated a moment, not sure where he was taking me. He typed a combination into a keypad on the door and swung it open, revealing a normal-looking office. I decided it was safe to follow him in, and he shut the door behind us.

"Take a seat." He gestured at one of the guest chairs sitting in front of the desk. He walked around it and settled in on a large leather chair on the other side. I picked the chair closest to the window and sat down. Todd rubbed his face with his hands.

"I'm lucky they let us open today," he said. "They had the parking lot all blocked off with crime-scene tape all day yesterday. I guess I'm lucky they found Joe first thing in the morning so they could get all their investigating over with in one day."

I was surprised by how mercenary his comments sounded, but I supposed it was reasonable to feel that way when your business and your livelihood were being affected.

He must have seen something in my face or realized how his comments could be interpreted because he quickly added, "A lot of people depend on me for their income, you know."

"Did they need to search inside the gym?" I asked. When Matt's dad had died, the police didn't realize it was murder until after the autopsy, so they didn't start out the investigation the same way they would have, had they known. I was curious about what they'd done when the cause of death was more obviously foul play.

"They did a basic search," he said. "Confiscated some trash bags and laundry. I had to go out and buy a bunch of new towels so people would have some to use in the showers and in the pool. They didn't dust for fingerprints or anything, though. Out in the parking lot though, man, I think they picked up every last rock that was out there. Cleanest the parking lot's ever been."

"Did they have to question people?" I asked.

He groaned and leaned back in his chair. "Every last person who works here! And now, they're working through all my members. I'll be lucky if they don't scare half of them off."

"Do you know if they have any leads yet? Any suspects?" I felt as though I was interrogating Todd, but I found it more than a little unnerving to think of a murderer wandering around town.

He looked me dead in the eye as he replied. "They have at least one."

"They do?" I asked. "Who?"

"Me."

Chapter Five

"What?" I shrieked, a little more loudly than I meant to. How on earth could they think Todd killed someone?

I realized in the next second that I'd spent precisely five minutes with him in the last fifteen years, which wasn't exactly enough to make a well-grounded character judgment. Still, he didn't seem like the kind of guy who would kill someone. He wasn't acting the way I imagined a murderer would act—he was calm, relaxed, flirty even!

"They questioned me for hours yesterday."

"It's your gym. Are you sure it's not just standard procedure? You know, to make sure they know about anything that could have led to... to the murder?" Even though Todd obviously knew what had happened just outside his office window, I still felt awkward saying "murder" in front of him. It wasn't something people got much practice discussing in polite conversation.

He shook his head. "Not with the questions they asked me." At first, he didn't elaborate, and even though I wanted to know, I didn't want to ask. Then he exhaled sharply and leaned forward, resting his elbows on his desk. He covered his face with his hands.

I sat still, not knowing what to do. Should I reach out and comfort him? Sit quietly until he gathered himself? Leave him in peace?

Before I could decide, he dropped his hands and looked at me, shaking his head. "You wouldn't even believe, Fran. Where was I every second of the day he died? Could anyone verify what I did? How well did I know Joe? For how long? How are the gym's finances? Did I have any kind of grudge against Joe? Could I tell them again where I was at nine o'clock? Who was working that day? Did I know if anyone had any issues with Joe? When was the last time I saw him? When did I expect to see him? How long has the gym been open? And it was like that, too—one question after another, on all different subjects, bouncing around from one thing to the next. I know they were trying to get me to slip up, but there was nothing to slip up about! And do you know how hard it is to remember exactly what you were doing at seven-fifty-five last night? And not to forget anything? I swear, I had to account for every breath I took."

He sounded frustrated and angry and, I think, even a little bit scared, not that I could blame him. Someone had been murdered in his parking lot, and he'd been interrogated—intensely, it sounded like. But the way he talked about it convinced me even more that he was innocent. Those questions the police had asked were designed to trip up someone who was lying. He didn't sound as though he'd had any problem keeping his story straight, and that had to count for something.

He leaned so far back in his chair that I thought he might fall over, and he let out a long, deep breath, his eyes fixed on the ceiling. "I don't know, Fran. I just don't even know."

I said the only thing I could think of. "I'm so sorry this is happening to you, Todd."

"Thank you," he said, leaning forward again. "And I'm sorry I dumped on you like that. I don't really know where all that came from. I guess I just had to get it off my chest. I don't have that many people I can talk to. Everyone here is my employee or my customer." He waved his hand expansively to indicate the gym. "I'm not going to tell my mom her son is a murder suspect. I live alone. You just happened to be in the right place at the right time. Not exactly a great way to say hello to an old friend, huh?"

There was that "friend" thing again. Did he just remember it differently than I did? Was I the one remembering it all wrong? Did he just consider everyone a friend? And why was I complaining about Todd Caruthers considering me a friend? Wouldn't I have died for that back in high school?

I chose to smile. "I'm glad I could be here when you needed me."

Todd flashed back his toothy white grin. His teeth practically glowed against his tanned skin. "So am I."

I felt warmth spread across my chest when he smiled at me like that. It made me feel like the homecoming queen.

"Now," Todd slapped his hand on the desk. "I know you didn't come here to listen to me go on about the cops asking me a million questions. What brought you out today?"

I tried to remember. Between getting lost in Todd's deep blue eyes and hearing about the murder, I'd virtually forgotten why I came. After an almost embarrassingly long pause, I noticed the same plastic display that had been on the reception desk sitting behind Todd.

"I wanted to see what kind of classes you have," I said. "What was her name—Karli?—she filled me in on all the different classes you offer, got me some brochures. I think she actually would have broken into a demonstration if you hadn't walked up when you did." I laughed so he knew I was kidding.

He laughed too. "Yeah, Karli's got some energy. She's great to have at the front desk. She really gets people in, makes them feel welcome, gets them raring to go." He paused and looked toward the papers in my lap. "Which brochures did she give you?" he asked.

I handed them over to him. He murmured as he flipped through.

"Yoga, Pilates, aerobics, dance, spin. Good stuff. We also have ballet barre and boot-camp classes you might like." He piled two more brochures onto my stack.

"I'm impressed how many different classes you have," I commented. "Honestly, I didn't expect there to be so many options in Cape Bay. We're not really known for being cutting edge here."

"Classes are one of my prime focuses," Todd said. "They're just the best way to get people in and get them moving. So many people come in, play around on the treadmill, get bored, and go home. Classes really get people engaged, get their blood flowing, keep them coming back. I actually pay a lot of attention to what they're doing in New York and LA. That's where the really exciting stuff comes from. I mean, who would have thought back when we were kids that stationary bikes would be the coolest workout on the planet? You can't see the trend until it hits, but when it hits, I want to be there. I want people to know that Todd's Gym is every bit as good as some fancy gym in the city."

I had never heard anyone speak so passionately about exercise classes. Well, some of the public relations girls I'd known back in New York talked about their spin classes with near-religious fervor, but Todd was different. He wasn't just obsessed with one particular class but with classes as a whole. I imagined his obsession was a little like the way I used to sound when I'd go on and on about coffee back before everyone and their brother was an "expert" on the subject. I'd always found that kind of passion deeply appealing in a person, even when I didn't understand the subject of their passion. I thought perhaps Todd and I could end up as real friends.

"That's awesome," I said. "I always liked trying different classes when I was back in the city. Some of them were just weird, but some of them were really amazing. I'd work out parts of my body I didn't even know I could work out!"

"See? That's what I love. People getting to do new things, move new ways. Not everyone is going to like every class, but just getting them to try it is a win. Man, I love that stuff!" He had a grin plastered on his face from ear to ear. "Hey, you know what else you should take?" He turned in his chair and pulled another brochure out of the rack to hand to me. "Kickboxing! Have you ever taken it? There are actually a lot of women who are really into it."

"Actually, I have," I replied. It hadn't been my thing. I could handle the kicks in a dance aerobics class or in a boot camp, but those were always air kicks. Kickboxing wanted you to kick something, even if it was just a punching bag. I didn't have that much aggression in me. "I didn't really like it."

"Oh, no?" The smile left Todd's face. Then he said, "Joe was a kickboxer."

"Professional?" I asked.

"Technically, yeah. He competed in the professional fights and got prize money, but he didn't make a living off of it. He was trying, though. He lost his job a few months back, so he was putting a lot more time into training. He was good. He had potential. He was getting a little old, but he was tough."

"Old? Wasn't he in his twenties?"

Todd chuckled. "Twenty-seven, yeah. Makes you feel *really* old, hearing that, doesn't it?"

I nodded. No wonder Karli had mentioned water aerobics to me.

"Me too," he continued. "Late twenties isn't old to be a fighter, but it's old to still be coming up. Most of the guys who are going to make something of themselves are going to start being known in their early twenties. It's just a couple of years, but it's enough to make a difference. Of course, a lot of them are going into MMA now."

"MMA?" I asked.

"Mixed Martial Arts. It's where you mix different styles of fighting instead of just following the rules of just one."

"Oh, that's the one where they look like they're trying to kill each other!" I had seen it on TV in the background at bars. It looked violent and bloody—also not my thing.

"Yeah, I guess it could look like that," Todd replied with a smile.

"Did Joe do MMA?"

"He was experimenting with it. He didn't have a background in any of the standard martial arts like a lot of these guys, so that put him behind, too. Poor kid. Couldn't catch a break."

I got the sense that Todd had a soft spot for Joe. "Did you know him well?" I asked.

"Yeah," he said. "He was a friend."

"I'm so sorry. This must be really hard for you."

"Thanks. It's tough. Between him being a friend and the impact on the gym's business and then waiting for the cops to break down my door and arrest me..." He exhaled. "Yeah, it's tough."

I instinctively reached my hand out across the desk toward him. He took it and squeezed. We sat there for a moment until I realized I was basically holding hands with Todd Caruthers. Even though it gave me a thrill, as soon as I was aware of it, I felt uncomfortable and pulled my hand away. I gave Todd a smile to make up for it.

"If there's anything I can do," I said, "please, let me know."

"Thank you, I will."

Just then, the phone on Todd's desk rang.

"Hang on, just a second, will you?" he said before picking it up. "Hello?" A pause. "Really?" He sighed. "Yeah, okay... Yeah... Tell them I'll be out in just a minute... okay... yeah... yeah... okay... bye." He put the phone down in its cradle and his head down in his hands.

"Everything okay?" I asked, knowing it wasn't.

"The cops are here. They want to talk to me."

"Again?"

"Again." He closed his eyes and took a deep breath. "Well, I guess we'll have to pick this up again later. Maybe I'll come by the coffee shop sometime? Assuming I'm not in jail."

"You won't be in jail!" I retorted, based solely on my own observances and not the years of police work and training that the detectives would be relying on.

"Let's hope," he replied, rising from the desk. He handed me the pile of brochures still sitting in front of him, and I added it to the kickboxing one in my hand. He walked around the desk and gave me a hug as though it was no big deal. I hugged him back because he was Todd Caruthers and my teenage self would have killed me if I didn't. "Thanks, Fran," he said, stepping away from me and toward the door. "You're a good friend." He pulled open the door, and I saw a small cluster of blue uniforms and black suits in the lobby.

"Come by the café sometime, and I'll buy you a cup of coffee," I said quietly as I walked past him.

"Thanks, I will," he replied. Then he addressed the police waiting for him. "Officers," he said. "If you'd like to come in..."

As they started to move into his office, I thought it would be a tight squeeze to fit all those broad shoulders inside Todd's office. It wasn't a particularly small room, but none of them were particularly small men either.

"Hello, Fran," one of the officers said.

I turned around and scanned their faces until I landed on the one who had spoken. Mike Stanton had been a classmate of mine and worked for the police department. Because the police department was small, he worked as a patrolman or a detective as necessary. Based on his black suit, I guessed he was a detective on that case. He'd been the detective on Matt's dad's murder case as well. I wondered if he was becoming Cape Bay's murder expert. I didn't think having a murder expert on the police force was something Cape Bay should necessarily be proud of.

"Hi, Mike," I said with a smile.

"You here catching up with an old friend?" he asked. There was that "friend" thing again. He sounded suspicious. Of course, the murder scene at the gym was the second he'd found me at or near, so I supposed that made sense. At least I hadn't been the one to find Joe's body.

I glanced back at Todd, who was still holding the door open, waiting for Mike to follow the rest of the officers. Todd gave me a grim smile.

"Yup," I said. I waved my hand around the large, open space. "And I wanted to see the gym. I didn't even know it was here until a couple of days ago."

Mike nodded. "Well, I'm sure I'll see you around." He didn't exactly sound pleased about that.

"See you!" I made it a point to sound as cheery as possible. I liked Mike. He was a good guy. My new knack for hanging around murder scenes just complicated that.

He nodded and stepped into Todd's office. I thought I saw a worried expression on Todd's face as he let the door close behind Mike. I hoped the conversation would go better than I knew he feared.

I caught Karli's eye as I turned to leave the gym. Her big blue eyes looked even bigger. She looked scared. If I were nineteen, my boss suspected of committing a murder, the victim of which was found practically where I parked my car every day, I would've been terrified. I felt a surge of sympathy for the girl.

"It'll be okay," I called softly to her.

She nodded but grabbed a tissue and turned her chair around to face away from the door.

I certainly hoped it would be okay.

Chapter Six

I had dinner with Matt that night. We went to a little authentic Italian restaurant in the next town. I'm generally suspicious of Italian places that claim to be authentic because most of the time, what they really mean is that they are authentic what-people-think-is-Italian. They are almost never right, partly because Italy is a big country with lots of different styles of food. The food in the north is, in a lot of ways, more like the food of Austria or France than it is like the food in Sicily. One size does not fit all. And a chef who is good at cooking one style isn't necessarily good at cooking another.

Osteria di Monica, though, was probably the most authentic I'd ever been to. My family had been eating there my entire life. The original owners had come over from Italy around the same time as my grandparents, after the war, and cooked exactly the same in the restaurant as they had back home. When their son was old enough, he went to culinary school. His parents were less than pleased with some of the "Italian" cooking methods he picked up there and sent him back to Venice, where they had emigrated from, for two years to learn how to cook proper Venetian food.

Presently, his son, the original owners' grandson, was now getting his full-immersion lesson in Italian cooking on his own two-year trip to Venice. He was due back in a little over six months, and the rumor was that he might be bringing a girl with him—a Venetian girl he'd met at the restaurant where he worked. The family could not have been more excited at the prospect of marrying off their boy and getting a new, properly-trained chef at the same time.

Matt and I studied our menus. We'd each been there easily over a hundred times, but they kept the menu seasonal, aside from a few staples, so we always wanted to look it over before deciding. We decided on carpaccio for an appetizer, then Matt ordered polenta with shrimp, and I chose risotto nero—a creamy rice dish colored black by cuttlefish ink. It wasn't an Americanized dish, that's for sure, and I'd certainly gotten some weird looks from people who found its color unusual and off-putting.

"So what's going on with you?" Matt asked after we ordered.

I looked at him curiously. "You know everything that's going on with me," I said. "I saw you yesterday."

"That's not what I mean," he replied. "What's going on? Why are you upset?"

I hadn't realized it was so obvious. I hesitated.

"Whatever it is, you can tell me, Franny."

I let out a long sigh. "I went over to Todd's Gym today."

"Hmm." Matt leaned back in his chair and crossed his arms over his chest. That seemed a strange reaction. I didn't know what else to do, so I went on.

"I just wanted to see what kind of classes they have."

"They have a website, you know."

I couldn't tell if he was being critical or factual. I didn't usually have so much trouble getting a read on Matt and wondered if he was upset about something too.

"I didn't think of that," I said honestly. "I guess I thought it would be too small and rinky-dink for that."

"No, he's pretty sophisticated about it."

"I noticed," I replied. "I know you said it was a big concrete square, but I didn't expect it to be that nice inside. And huge. It's huge!"

"Yeah, he went all out with that place," he replied with a chuckle. His posture seemed to relax. "Is that what bothered you? That you went over there and the place was nice?"

"No." For some reason, my worry felt personal, and even though I was close to Matt, I was conflicted about telling him what was on my mind.

"Then what?"

I blurted it out. "They suspect Todd of Joe's murder."

Matt paused as he appeared to think this over. Then: "And it bothers you that he's a suspect or that he may be a murderer?"

The difference between the two options was almost insignificant, but I understood what he was really asking—did I think Todd was guilty or innocent? I didn't have a doubt in my mind.

"Todd didn't kill Joe."

"I wasn't saying he did," Matt replied. "I just wanted to understand what was bothering you." I could see the sincerity in his face.

"I know. I just... It's been a long day. I didn't go out there expecting to see Todd, and then there he was, just out of the blue. I didn't even think he'd remember me, but he did. And he was so thoughtful, asking about how I was doing since my mom passed away—and you! He asked about how you've been doing since your dad's murder."

"Todd Caruthers asked about me?" Matt asked.

"Yes!" I replied. "He seemed different from the way he was back in high school. He was polite and thoughtful. I was really surprised."

Matt considered that information, though he seemed not to believe me. "So you don't think he's a murderer because he was nice to you, a pretty girl." Matt's tone was so flat and even that it took me a second to realize what he'd said.

"You think I'm pretty?" I asked with a smile. He'd mentioned it in such an offhand way, I almost laughed.

"Of course I do." He scoffed. "And I'm sure Todd does, too. He has eyes, doesn't he?"

Stunning blue ones. "Yes, I seem to recall eyes."

"Well then, he's seen you, and he knows you're pretty. And guys tend to be nice to pretty girls." He was an odd combination of flirty and combative—calling me pretty one second and dismissing Todd the next. He really was in a strange mood.

The waitress brought our appetizer, and I took the opportunity to change the subject.

"So, how's work?" I asked as we cut into the thin slices of beef.

"It's good."

"Just 'it's good'?" I laughed.

"Oh, you know. Same old, same old."

"Any new and interesting projects?"

"Actually, there is one. There's a big private university down in Virginia that wants to completely revamp their network—everything from how the school's network connects to the Internet all the way to how students and staff access the network. It's huge—a million moving parts. We just signed the contract with them this morning, and it'll probably be a year before we make any physical changes on the campus and another two or three years after that before we're done."

"Wow," I said. It was a simplistic response, but only because I could only barely understand what Matt did for a living. I knew he was a project manager for telecom engineering. I knew that, in addition to projects, he also managed several engineers. I knew they were all good at their jobs and fairly self-sufficient, but Matt's job was the one on the line if they ever screwed up. He worked on several projects at a time and was one of his firm's top engineers, getting sent out across the country to work on their highest-priority jobs.

"Yeah, I have to fly down early next week to meet with them and have the project kickoff meeting."

"You're going out of town?" Because of his father's death, Matt had taken some time off from travelling for work and hadn't been out of town since we'd reconnected. We had spent so much time together over the past few weeks that I wasn't sure what I would do on my own. I was glad I would have Latte to keep me company.

"Yup," he confirmed. "It's been kind of nice sleeping in my own bed the past few weeks. It's going to be kind of strange getting back out on the road again."

I had never traveled for work like Matt did—just some conferences here and there when I worked in public relations back in the city. I couldn't imagine what it was like to spend so much time on the road.

"I don't know how you do it," I said. "I don't think I could."

"You get used to it," he replied with a shrug. "I get to see a lot of parts of the country I probably wouldn't otherwise."

"I feel like I would get bored spending all that time in hotel rooms."

"I usually get to sightsee a little. There are only so many hours of the day you can be in meetings. I mean, when else are you going to find yourself in a position to go to the Zippo lighter museum?"

"There's a Zippo lighter museum?"

"Yup, right there at the factory. It's actually a pretty cool place." He paused and smiled. "And I never would have gotten to see it if I wasn't bored and alone on the road."

I had to laugh. He had a point there.

"What else have you seen?"

"You want weird, quirky stuff or the serious museums and national landmarks?"

"Oh, definitely the quirky stuff. You can go to an art museum just about anywhere. I want the one-of-a-kind stuff."

He thought for a moment. "Um, lots of presidential birthplaces, but those are on the more serious side. The world's largest teapot. A life-size chocolate moose. The most historic alley in Delaware."

I interrupted him. "Wait, what happened there? What makes it so historic?"

He fought back a smile. "The riverboats offloaded at one end of the alley, and the stagecoaches picked up at the other end. Lots of important figures in history walked along that alley to get from the riverboats to the stagecoaches."

I looked at him for a few seconds, judging how serious he was being. The tale sounded like something he could very well be making up.

"How do you know it's so historic?" I asked.

"The plaque they had posted there told me."

I burst out laughing and had to cover my mouth with my hand to stop myself from disturbing the whole restaurant. There was something extremely entertaining to me about the idea that a state had gone to the trouble to erect a plaque to commemorate where some historical figures had once walked.

Matt was trying to restrain his laughter as well. I wasn't sure whether he thought the alley was as funny as I did or my laughter was making him laugh along. Either way, the two of us were cracking up when the waitress brought over our meals and set them in front of us.

Matt's polenta was thick and creamy, with a generous helping of shrimp piled on top. My risotto was black as night, with chunks of cuttlefish mixed into it. We both calmed our laughter down enough to start eating, although I convinced Matt to continue his stories about interesting places he had visited in his travels around the country. I even got to hear all about a museum he visited that was devoted entirely to art and artifacts related to death and mourning. It was an unusual premise for a museum to be built on, but according to what Matt said, it was a really nice museum and an interesting place. I told him I'd take his word for it.

We decided to split a dessert since neither of us was very hungry after our full meals. Any other time, we probably would have skipped it, but Osteria di Monica has the most delicious desserts. We ordered the tiramisu because, in my opinion, it's the best of all. Setting aside all the rest of the food, I would go there just for that.

When it arrived, I sat and looked at it for a moment, admiring its beauty and anticipating all the flavors.

"What are you waiting for?" Matt asked, his fork poised over the dish.

"Nothing," I said and plunged my own fork in. The tiramisu was every bit as delicious as I had expected—maybe even more. I sometimes wondered if it was possible to remember something that good accurately or if you always convinced yourself that you were remembering it through rose-colored glasses. There weren't many things that were better than I remembered, but this always seemed to be one of them. Either that or it actually got better every time.

"Oh my God, Franny," Matt said.

I momentarily wondered if he'd forgotten that I wasn't the one who made the dessert.

"This is so good! You know, you should serve tiramisu at the café. It's Italian and has a lot of coffee in it, just like you." His eye gleamed as he said it. "You're a great baker. I bet you could make something every bit as good as this, if not better."

"I don't know about that," I said, taking another bite. It really was exquisite. The flavors were perfectly balanced, and the texture was everything I would want it to be. Putting something together that well took skill and practice, even with a no-bake recipe. Still, his comment gave me an idea.

"How was it?" the waitress asked, coming by a few minutes later to drop off the check.

"Amazing!" I answered.

"The best thing I've ever eaten," Matt said. Then to me: "No offense, Fran."

"None taken," I replied sincerely.

"Great!" the waitress chirped. "Is there anything else I can get you?"

"Actually, would it be possible for us to speak to the chef?" I asked.

"Sure!" she replied. "I'll go get him." She laid the bill down on the table. "And I'll take that whenever you're ready."

Matt grabbed the check before I could even make a move for it. I gave him a dirty look.

The chef, the son of the original owners, came out moments later. He was a tall man with dark hair and olive skin.

"Matteo! Francesca! How are my two favorite customers?" He was exaggerating, of course. I was reasonably certain he greeted all regulars that way.

We exchanged pleasantries, and I asked how his son Stefano was doing in Italy. He gushed about how much Stefano was learning and how much they were looking forward to his return. The young lady that Stefano was expected to bring back with him received a fair bit of enthusiasm as well.

"How was everything?" Alberto asked when we were all caught up. "Did everything taste good?"

"Everything was delicious," I said. "That's actually sort of what I wanted to talk to you about. Is your mom still making the tiramisu?"

"She is, yes, with my wife helping also. Was there a problem with it?"

"No, no, no! Not at all. It was amazing!" I said hurriedly. His face was covered with curiosity, so I just went ahead and asked my next question. "You know I'm running Antonia's now, right?"

"Of course." He was still baffled.

"What would you think of selling your tiramisu in my café? It's so good—I know people would buy it, and I bet you would get new customers out of it, too."

I could tell he had never thought about selling his food off-site. But dessert—tiramisu especially—was a different animal than risotto. It could be made ahead of time. It could keep for several hours or even days.

"We could start small," I told him, sensing his indecision. "Maybe five or ten pieces? You set the price, and we can split the profits—fifty-fifty, sixty-forty, whatever you want. Monica's doing the work of making it. I just have to put it in my display case, and it'll sell itself."

Alberto crossed his arms across his chest as he thought over my offer.

"Let me talk to my mother. And my wife. We'll see what they think, if they want to make more each day. If they say yes, then it's a deal."

"Great!" I replied. "I hope it works out. And if it doesn't, no hard feelings. I'll be back here to eat every week anyway."

He laughed. "Oh, I know you will!"

Matt and I expressed our thanks for the exceptional meal and said our goodbyes as Alberto went back to the kitchen.

"I didn't see that coming," Matt said. "When did you decide you were going to ask him that?"

"When you suggested I sell tiramisu at Antonia's."

"I suggested you make it. You're an amazing baker."

"Well, thank you." I smiled. "But Monica's been perfecting her tiramisu recipe for years. It's the best I've ever tasted. Why try to improve upon perfection?"

"Your coffee's pretty perfect, and you're always trying to improve on that."

"That's because it's *mine*. You should always try to improve on yourself. But I don't have to be the best at everything. I'm perfectly happy letting Monica be the best at tiramisu."

"Well, I'm glad I gave you the idea," Matt replied with a smile.

I laughed at his effort to take credit for something he could barely argue he had suggested. "Thank you for that," I said through my laughter.

After Matt finished paying, we walked out to his car. He usually drove when we went places because he liked to drive about as much as I didn't. I was excited about the possibility of selling Monica's tiramisu in my café, but once we were in the darkness of the car, with only the road ahead of me to focus on, my mind drifted back to my morning visit to Todd's Gym and the revelation that he was a suspect in Joe's murder. That did bother me, mostly because I didn't think he'd done it. I realized that if I was able to find out who had killed Matt's dad, maybe I could use those same investigative skills to help Todd by finding out who had really killed Joe.

Chapter Seven

"You doing all right over there?" Matt asked after a few minutes.

"Hmm?" I responded. His question had barely penetrated my thoughts.

"I asked if you're all right over there. You've been awfully quiet since we got in the car."

"Oh. Yeah." I stared out the window. Based on Matt's reaction earlier when I brought up the subject of Todd, I wasn't sure I wanted to mention him again, especially not my idea of helping him.

"Thinking about Joe's murder again?"

I looked over at Matt in surprise. I hadn't expected him to guess what was going on in my head. "Yes," I admitted. "It just bothers me that the police seem to have jumped on him so readily without doing much investigating."

"I'm sure they have their reasons."

"I know. I just—" I stopped and sighed. I wasn't the kind of person who doubted the police, since I generally assumed they knew what they were doing. Still, Todd being a suspect didn't sit right with me. He didn't *feel* like someone who could commit murder, and I was fairly certain that wasn't just because I thought he was good looking. He didn't talk like a murderer or act like a murderer. He talked and acted like a guy who was freaked out about being a murder suspect and having his livelihood on the line due to a murder having taken place in his business's parking lot. "I just don't think he did it," I said finally.

Matt was quiet. I worried that he was upset with me.

After a few minutes, he said quietly, "You know, you're the one who found out who killed my dad. You did a good job with that—finding evidence, figuring out what you needed to investigate next. As long as you don't get in the way of the police investigation, maybe it wouldn't hurt to do it again. Even if you don't figure out who else might have done it, you might be able to find enough evidence to know whether or not it was Todd." He glanced away from the road and over at me, then back at the road. He shrugged. "You know, if you wanted to."

I couldn't believe Matt had come to the same conclusion I had. Not only that—he was actually suggesting it.

"You really think it's a good idea?" I asked.

"Only if it's something you feel like you want to do. I'm not saying you have to or that Todd's life is in your hands or anything. I'm sure the police will figure it out sooner or later. But if it makes you feel better to look into it on your own, I don't see what it could hurt."

"I was actually thinking the same thing," I said.

"You were?" He sounded surprised.

"Yeah, I mean, if I did it once, I can do it again, right? And now I actually have some practice with it. I think I could do it. I think I could help Todd."

"I could help you if you want," Matt offered.

"Really?" I asked. "You would do that for me?" I hadn't expected that. Matt had been a huge help to me in solving his father's murder, and I couldn't have done it without him, but I hadn't anticipated him offering to help me investigate a murder that had nothing to do with him.

"Sure. I don't want you running around, chasing a murderer on your own—you could get hurt again."

He had a point. My last investigation had proven dangerous, and I still had twinges of pain every once in a while. That didn't stop me from wanting to do it again, though.

"Thank you!" I replied with a smile. I wanted to throw my arms around him and give him a big hug, but I didn't think that was a wise move while he was driving. I realized I would have to save it for later. For the moment, I focused on plotting out how I was going to get started.

"I think I'll go see Todd again," I said.

"You will?" Matt asked, sounding surprised again.

I wondered if that was just a result of him being focused on driving.

"Yes, I think I will. When we talked this morning, it was just chitchat, catching up on what was going on. I don't know what kind of evidence the police have against him or anything. I won't know what to look for if I don't know what evidence they have already."

Matt didn't say anything. My mind was whirling, so I kept talking. Thinking out loud would at least keep Matt in the loop on where my brain was going.

"I almost think he's not actually a suspect—that the police are just doing their job and questioning him thoroughly because the body was found in his parking lot—and he just thinks he is. It makes sense that the police would need to talk to him a lot. It doesn't necessarily mean he's a suspect, right?"

Matt stayed quiet.

"Matt?"

"Yeah."

I couldn't tell if that was a statement or a question, whether he was agreeing with me or hadn't been listening, so I repeated myself. "The police questioning Todd a lot doesn't necessarily mean he's a suspect, right? They may just be covering their bases?"

"I don't know. I'm not a cop."

I heaved a sigh. "Well, I know that. I'm just asking your opinion."

"I think it looks suspicious," he said. "And he said that they consider him a suspect. I don't know why he would think that if he's not. But it's always possible that he's wrong. Or they're wrong. Every cop show I've ever seen goes through a list of suspects before they catch the guy who did it."

It was a levelheaded response, weighing the possibilities. I would have liked his reply better if he'd come down solidly on the side of Todd probably not actually being a suspect, but I had to respect his honesty and logical approach. Besides, it would be good for our investigation, for him to have such a reasoned approach to balance my more instinctual one.

"I guess you're right," I admitted. "But that still means I need to figure out what the evidence is so I know how to prove that he's innocent."

"Or guilty," Matt added. "He could be guilty."

I looked at him, but I couldn't read his expression in the darkness of the car. "He could be," I agreed. "I don't think he is, but he could be." As much as I wanted to prove that Todd was not the murderer, finding out who really killed Joe was more important. Letting a murderer walk the streets was unacceptable.

We were almost home by then, just crossing into Cape Bay. Todd's Gym was on our left as we drove in, its bright yellow sign gleaming in the night. Light poured out of the large front entryway, and the parking lot was lit up as bright as day.

"Are they still open?" I asked Matt.

"Yup," he replied. "Twenty-four hours."

"Really? A twenty-four-hour gym in Cape Bay? How did I not know about this? Does it have enough business to support it?"

"I guess so. I think he gets people from some of the neighboring towns and some shift workers. And I think the fighting is at night."

"The fighting?" I gasped.

"I mean boxing. Kickboxing, MMA, whatever they do there."

"Oh," I breathed with relief. "I thought you meant fight-club kind of fighting!"

Matt laughed. "No, but have you seen that MMA stuff? It's not far off."

"Mm-hmm," I murmured, nodding even though he couldn't see me. There was a thought playing at the back of my mind. I knew it was important, but I couldn't quite catch it. And then I did. "Wait, is the parking lot always that bright, or is it just because of Joe?"

"It's always that bright," Matt replied.

"So whoever killed him did it in a brightly lit parking lot, and then he was right there where anybody could see him until the morning. That's weird, isn't it?"

"All murder is weird in a way, isn't it?"

"I guess so," I said. Still, the murder having taken place in such a brightly lit place seemed strange to me, and I realized that, in addition to finding any evidence against Todd, I also had to discover more about the murder itself—all I knew was that Joe had been stabbed to death. I needed to know who found him and when he was last seen and probably a lot more that I hadn't thought about yet. So many thoughts were racing through my head that I was getting antsy to get home and start writing them down so I wouldn't forget anything. Fortunately, Matt was turning the car onto our street.

He parked in his driveway. "I'll walk you home," he said. We cut across our neighbor's yard, and Matt waited until I had unlocked the door and Latte had shot out between us before he hugged me good night.

"Don't spend too much time thinking about this Todd thing, okay?" he said.

"I won't," I replied. I planned to think about it a good bit before I went to sleep, but "too much" was a relative concept, and I didn't feel as though the thinking I had planned quite qualified.

Matt waved and headed back across the grass toward his house.

"Come here, Latte!" I called. He ran past me into the house and danced around my feet as I locked up, waiting for me to pet him. I knelt down and rubbed his ears vigorously for a minute, and then we headed upstairs.

I picked up a yellow legal pad from my dresser, flipped to a blank page, and sat down with it on the edge of my bed. I jotted down a series of notes about what I wanted to know:

What evidence do they have against Todd?

Who found Joe's body?

Where in the parking lot was it found?

Who last saw him?

Did anyone have a grudge against Joe?

And so on and so on. Every question that crossed my mind, I added to the list. I had almost a full page by the time I was finished, from the biggest, broadest, most general questions—Who *killed Joe?*—down to the most detailed—Where *did the murderer get the weapon?* I didn't know how I was going to get answers to all of them or even if I would, but I felt my list was enough to guide me as I got started.

I glanced at the clock. Between closing the café, having dinner with Matt, and making my list of questions, time flew until it was well after midnight. I needed to get to bed if I was going to get up and go back to the gym in the morning to try talking to Todd. I quickly changed my clothes and got ready for bed and then snuggled between my sheets with Latte, as usual, curled up at my feet. I fell asleep almost immediately.

Chapter Eight

I woke up in the morning with Latte nudging me for his breakfast and morning walk. He was hungry, and I had slept later than usual. I stumbled downstairs and fed him and then went back upstairs to get dressed while he ate.

I needed to go straight to work after visiting Todd, so I put my work clothes on—black pants and a black top, despite the heat—and put my hair up in a ponytail. Latte was waiting for me at the bottom of the stairs when I came back down. I hooked his leash on, and we headed outside.

Our morning walk is usually the longest. I usually come home from the café a couple of times throughout the day for a few minutes to take him out and play, and then we take a walk around the block every evening. In the morning, though, sometimes we'll walk all the way out to the beach so Latte can play in the waves for a few minutes. On our good days, we'll go a couple of miles, walking all around town. That day, though, we didn't go that far, and I promised him we'd go out longer when I got home that night. Once Latte was all taken care of and safely back in the house, I walked to Todd's Gym.

I mentally reviewed the notes I'd made the night before as I walked, preparing myself to see Todd. The legal pad was tucked away in my purse, which was rather large. Every so often, I try to downsize and carry fewer items, but that only ever lasts a week or two before I find myself back to using the bigger bag.

I just found it so much more convenient to be able to carry around tissues and pain killers and extra makeup and pens and whatever else I might need with me at all times. Back in my stiletto-wearing New York City days, I'd even been known to carry an extra pair of shoes in my purse for when the heels started to kill my feet. Being back home in Cape Bay and working on my feet in the café all day had reminded me of the pleasure of flats and relegated my stilettos to the back of my closet. The large purse was still convenient for when I needed to tote around a legal pad, though.

I arrived at Todd's Gym and was again impressed by its size. One wouldn't realize, without standing right there by it, how incredibly large it was. The parking lot was fuller than I'd expected it to be in the middle of a weekday. I looked around before I went through the big glass doors into the foyer, trying to guess where in the parking lot Joe had been found. Nothing I could see seemed to indicate where that might have been, so I went on inside.

Perky, blond Karli was sitting at the reception desk again, her hair still in that impossibly high ponytail. I wondered how her scalp didn't hurt.

She waved, apparently recognizing me from the day before. "Hi! Welcome back! How are you today?"

"I'm good." I smiled, approaching the desk and reaching my hand across it. "You're Karli, right? I'm Fran."

"Hi, Fran!" she replied, taking my hand and shaking hesitantly. I got the feeling she didn't do much handshaking at her age or in her job.

"Is Todd in?" It hadn't occurred to me until that very moment that I probably should have called before I came over in case he was out or busy.

Karli opened her mouth to say something, glanced at Todd's office door, and then closed it again. "Yes," she said after a few more seconds. "But he's with the police."

"The police?" I repeated, a little louder than I meant to.

Karli nodded furiously.

"Again?"

She nodded again.

"How long have they been in there?"

She glanced at the clock on her computer screen. "An hour, maybe?" she said softly, almost as though afraid they would hear her across the huge foyer, through the door, and over whatever conversation they were having.

"Wow." I glanced over at the door. He must be a serious suspect if they were back yet again and talking to him for such a long time. But they hadn't arrested him or even taken him down to the police station, so maybe it wasn't that bad after all. "How long were they here yesterday?"

She shrugged. "I'm not sure. A while."

That wasn't particularly helpful. I looked toward the door again and wondered if waiting was worthwhile. I figured the morning would be wasted if I didn't get to talk to Todd, but I'd be kicking myself if I found out the police left only a few minutes after I did. I sighed and drummed my fingers on the counter. I looked back at Karli. "Think I should wait?"

Before she could say anything, a lock clicked, and Todd's office door swung open. I turned, and Mike was the first one out the door. We made eye contact briefly before I looked away. Mike said nothing, just continuing out the front door with his fellow officers trailing behind him, one dressed in a suit like Mike's, the other two in uniform. Todd appeared in the doorway after them, haggard and exhausted. He looked over toward the reception desk and caught sight of me.

He pushed a smile onto his face and started across the lobby toward me.

"Hey, Franny," he called, his cheerful demeanor the polar opposite of what it had been moments earlier as the police left his office. "You here to sign up for some classes?"

"Nope, I'm here to see you," I replied.

"Really?" I saw his smile switch from the fake business-owner one it had been to a genuine one. "To what do I owe the pleasure?"

"Could we talk in your office?" I asked.

"Sure thing!" He looked past me. "Karli, hold my calls, please."

"Okay!" she chirped.

I wondered how many calls he got but then considered that he probably had a fair number of suppliers and support people calling him, not to mention clients who were wondering whether the gym was open and safe after what had happened to Joe.

In Todd's office, I took the same seat I'd had the day before, and he again sat in his chair on the other side of the desk.

"So, what's up, Franny?" he asked.

I noticed he always called me "Franny," which I'd gone by in high school. I supposed that wasn't very different from my tendency to call Matt "Matty."

"The police were here again," I stated.

He sighed and sank into his chair. I caught a glimpse of the worn-down expression he'd had on his face earlier. "Yep, they were back," he sighed, staring down at the desk.

"Third time?"

"Yep."

"Are you still a suspect?"

"More than ever, I think."

"Why?" I asked. The question burst through my lips before I had a chance to stop it. I hadn't meant to ask that way.

Todd looked up at me with an expression that was equal parts confused and surprised.

"Sorry, that came out wrong." I took a deep breath. "Todd, I want to help you. I don't quite know why it is, but I don't think you're a murderer."

"Maybe because I'm not?" he interjected.

I smiled. "That could be one reason. But if you really didn't do it, there has to be some kind of evidence, some proof that you didn't. Or, failing that, that someone else did. And I want to find it. I want to find it to get you off the hook and get justice for Joe and Joe's family. But I need your help to do that. Before I can do anything else, I need to know what they have against you." I almost got out my notepad but feared he would feel as though I was interrogating him. I decided I would just talk to him and write down my notes as soon as I got outside.

Todd stared at me critically, as if trying to see whether or not I was lying. He either gave up or decided I was telling the truth because he exhaled and shook his head. "Not much," he said. "Circumstantial. They have more evidence of where I *wasn't* and what I *wasn't* doing than what I was."

"What *weren't* you doing?" I asked.

"Most importantly to them, I wasn't doing anything I can prove. And I wasn't doing it with anyone who can tell them that I was doing it."

Though it might have been awkward, I had to ask the obvious question. "Were you doing it with someone who *can't* tell them? Or doesn't want to? Because maybe it was something she wasn't supposed to be doing?"

Todd looked at me incredulously, apparently not believing I was asking him what he thought I was asking. I deliberately kept an innocent look on my face. Todd finally laughed, hard and loud. "No," he said, regaining his composure. "I was home alone, watching TV. Probably the most normal thing I could do, but it's the most suspicious to the cops."

"Is that the only reason they suspect you, or is there something else?"

He took a deep breath. "It's my gym, and he was killed here and found here."

That reminded me. "Oh yeah, he was found in the parking lot, right? Where in the parking lot? I drove by last night with Matt, and the place was lit up like it was daytime."

"Yeah, that was to make it safe since it's open twenty-four hours." He scoffed. "So much for that."

I waited a moment to see if he was going to answer my question and then, when it was apparent he wasn't, I reminded him of my question. "Where in the parking lot was he found?"

"The side lot. There aren't as many lights there. I didn't think there needed to be, with how bright the front and back lots were. Who knows if that would have made a difference, though? If somebody wanted him dead, some lights weren't necessarily going to stop them."

"Do you think someone wanted him dead?" I asked. Somehow, that question hadn't occurred to me before. It wasn't even on my legal-pad list.

"Cape Bay's not exactly a hotbed of crime," he said dryly.

"True," I replied. "So do you know anybody who had it in for him?"

"No. Not really. I mean, the fighters tend to all leave it in the ring. They beat the crap out of each other, and then it's over. They walk away, and they're done. All that aggression stays in the ring."

"He was stabbed anyway, wasn't he?" I figured a kickboxing grudge would've been settled by more kickboxing.

"With a piece of glass." Todd scoffed.

"Really?"

"Yeah, trust me, I got the third degree from the cops on that one, too. I can't keep the kids from coming out here and drinking beer and leaving their bottles in the parking lot to get broken. I have a million lights out there. I don't know what else they want me to do."

"How does a piece of glass give you a wound deep enough to kill you?" I asked. It was a gruesome question, but I had to know.

"Apparently, it punctured his heart or something. Cops said it was either an accident or the guy knew what he was doing. They grilled me on how much I knew about anatomy, whether I'd taken any biology classes in college or anything."

"And did you?"

"What? You think I did it?" He sounded a little defensive.

I realized I might have been getting a little too aggressive in my questioning. "No, of course not! I just want to know what they know. Really, I want to help you, Todd."

"Of course I did," he said, giving in. "I was an exercise-science major. We took practically as much anatomy as the pre-med majors."

"I have a few more questions if that's okay."

"Go ahead. I'd rather talk to you than the cops again." Based on how unhappy he sounded about talking to me anymore, he must have been really unenthusiastic about talking to the police.

"Who found Joe's body?" I asked.

"Cleaning crew. They come in overnight when things are slower and leave around five in the morning. That's when they found him."

"Was he here before that?"

"Yeah, he was with his trainer."

"Was he here every Monday?"

"Every Monday." I was starting to detect some hostility in Todd's voice. I didn't blame him, though—he'd been through a lot the past few days.

"What about security cameras?" I asked. A big, fancy place like Todd's Gym seemed like it should be wired up with security cameras covering every inch. In fact, I was pretty sure I'd seen the cameras, both in the parking lot and inside the gym. I couldn't imagine the police hadn't already asked the question, but if they had, they would have made an arrest by now, and we wouldn't have been sitting there discussing it.

"Don't ask." Todd shook his head.

"That makes it sound like I do need to ask."

"They're not working."

I raised an eyebrow, realizing why he didn't want me to ask.

"It's something with the software," he continued. "I don't really get it. My IT guy explained it, but all I really got was that there's a problem with the software. They're supposed to be motion activated so we don't use a ton of storage space or something, but something about the calibration or the servers or something... I don't know. The guy's been working on it for like a month and keeps saying he's got it figured out, but apparently not."

I understood why that made the police suspicious. A big fancy security system like that conveniently not working—no wonder Todd was a suspect. At least he had the IT guy to vouch for him that the system had been down for a while.

"Is there anything else you can tell me? Anything that can point me to who else might have done it?"

"I don't know, Franny." He shook his head. "Joe was a friend of mine. I want his killer in jail. I don't know who it was, but it wasn't me. That's all I know. That's all I can tell you."

"Well, thanks," I said. "I'll get out of your hair now." I scooted to the front of my chair, ready to get up.

Todd sighed. "I'm sorry if I've been kind of a jerk. It's just been a rough week."

"It's no problem," I said with a smile.

Todd stood up and came around the desk to give me a hug good-bye. I was impressed again with how strong his arms were. He opened the door to let me out. "Come by anytime," he said. "Or maybe we could get dinner sometime."

"That'd be fun!" I said. I waved good-bye and went outside. Some benches were in front of the gym, and I sat down on one to think about what Todd had told me and to write everything down.

The gym was Todd's, he knew Joe, he knew there were broken beer bottles in the parking lot, he had a knowledge of anatomy, and he didn't have an alibi. I understood why the police suspected him. If I was going to prove that Todd hadn't done it—and I still believed he was innocent—I had my work cut out for me. I was going to have to find more suspects.

Chapter Nine

I was at the café with Sammy that afternoon, finally getting the chance to go through my box of tea. I had ordered everything from our supplier that I'd ever heard of before, everything that looked interesting, and everything the supplier's website recommended, based on other people's purchases.

Even though I was the one who had placed the order, I was surprised by the sheer number of boxes and tins I was pulling out of the shipping box. Earl Grey, Darjeeling, English breakfast, Irish breakfast, Scottish breakfast, black, green, white, oolong, rooibos, chai, chamomile, peppermint, herbal. I had loose leaf, square teabags, round teabags, pyramid teabags. I even had silk sachets of tea that I fully recognized were in no way practical for use in the café.

The table in the back room was completely covered when I heard the jingle of the bell over the front door. I angled my head so I could see who it was and how many there were so I would know if Sammy needed my help out front. The visitor was just Mike, so I went back to my teas.

I decided to organize them by how the tea was contained—loose versus types of teabag. I wanted to compare how the flavors of one tea were different in each form. What I'd seen online basically told me that loose leaves would give the best flavor, then the pyramids, then the flat teabags, but I wanted to see for myself. I also had to figure out which was the most practical for use in the café.

I could hear Mike and Sammy talking out front and Sammy making his drink. No matter what I was doing in the back room—sorting through shipments, paying bills, balancing the books—I always liked to keep an ear out for what was going on in the main part of the café. I could tell how things were going by the clink of cups and saucers, the hissing of the espresso machine, the murmur of conversation, and the jingle of the bell on the door.

Sammy had more than once been impressed with how I'd popped out of the back exactly when she needed an extra pair of hands. That was a skill I'd picked up when I used to do my homework in the back while my mother or grandparents worked out front. Mike and Sammy were just bantering happily, so I knew everything was under control.

I separated the Earl Grey teas into a different pile. It wasn't possible to find all the different forms of tea from one brand, but Earl Grey was common enough that I was able to get all of them from just two. I even got the loose tea from both brands so I could compare them.

I had brought a couple French presses from home so I could prepare the loose teas simultaneously without mixing the flavors of the different brands. I pulled them out of my massive purse and found a space for them on the tea-covered desk. I pulled out the teaspoons I had packed in my bag and was getting ready to measure some tea into each French press to start my first test when I heard a rap on the doorframe.

"Franny? Can I talk to you for a minute?"

I looked up to see Mike standing in the doorway and immediately felt a wave of dread wash over me.

I forced myself to sound cheery. "Hey Mike, sure. Come on in!" There was always a chance Mike could be there on a social call. I pushed a rolling chair toward him.

Mike came in and sat down. I took another chair, trying not to look nervous.

"What's up?" I asked.

"Just wanted to come by and say hello, see how you're doing," he replied.

"I'm doing pretty well. And yourself?" I tried to disguise my suspicion with politeness. The last time I'd been in a small room with Detective Mike Stanton, he hadn't been too happy with me.

"I'm all right. Got another murder case."

"I heard." So the conversation was going where I'd thought.

"So I guess you also heard the victim was found in the parking lot of Todd's Gym?"

"I did." I thought it best to keep my answers brief at that point.

"I couldn't help but notice you've been over at the gym the last couple of times I've been there to talk to Todd. Any reason that is?"

I was glad he didn't have his notebook out, scribbling down notes about our conversation. "Yesterday, I was over there to find out about what classes they offered. I'd like to take a couple when the busy season is over."

"You could have checked their website, you know," Mike replied.

Again with the website! Weren't people these days always complaining about how no one ever wanted to talk face-to-face anymore?

"Matt said the same thing," I said, figuring Mike didn't want to hear all that.

"Matt's a smart man."

"I honestly didn't think they would have a website." I decided to give Mike more of an explanation. "Especially not one with that information. It's Cape Bay. We're not usually that sophisticated."

Mike chuckled. "I'll give you that. But, Fran, I have to ask, I saw you coming out of Todd Caruthers' office. I can't believe he meets individually with everyone who comes in to see what classes his gym offers—behind closed doors in his office, no less."

"Just what are you insinuating?" I asked, incredulously, my voice rising a little further than I probably should have let it.

"I'm not insinuating anything. I'm just saying—it seems like you were there for more than information on classes."

"That's why I went there," I said. "I talked to the girl at the desk—"

"Karli," Mike prompted.

"Karli," I repeated after him. "I talked to Karli, and she gave me a bunch of brochures, and as I was talking to her, Todd came up to the desk. I hadn't seen him since high school. We started talking. It was no big deal."

"And how did you end up back in his office?"

"Am I being interrogated?" I asked, suddenly wondering if, despite the lack of a notebook, there really was something more to this conversation than a friendly chat.

Mike held up both hands in a gesture of surrender. "No, no, no. Sorry. I get a little too used to asking people questions, and I forget that's not how normal people talk.

My wife always gives me grief about it. Tells me I'm interrogating her when she's just trying to tell me about her day at work."

I knew his wife—she'd gone to high school with all of us—and I could just picture her going off on Mike about something like that. "Well, I guess if it's the same treatment you give Sandra, I can't complain about it too much." I laughed.

Mike chuckled along with me. "A'right," he said after a few moments. "So, I'm not going to grill you on how exactly you ended up back in Todd's office because it's probably—hopefully—none of my business, but I will say that I want you to be careful. I don't know who killed Joe Davis, but I know someone's not telling me the truth. I'm going to find out what happened, and I don't want you getting caught in the middle of it when it all goes down. And if you're thinking about undertaking another independent investigation like you did with Gino Cardosi, I'm going to go ahead and advise you against it."

I opened my mouth to protest, but Mike held up a hand to stop me.

"I know you solved the case, but you put yourself and other people in danger doing it. I don't want that happening again. You need to stay out of it. Do you understand?" Mike's tone had changed from friendly and amenable to stern and police-like.

"Okay," I said, simply. Whether I agreed with him or not, there was no use arguing.

"Okay!" he replied, accepting my answer and slapping his hands on his knees. "Now, I think Sammy probably has some coffee ready for me."

Sammy came through the door holding a to-go coffee cup with a protective cardboard sleeve wrapped around it. I wondered how much of our conversation she had heard and if she'd been listening at the door. "Here you go. One large coffee, black."

"Mike, I think Sammy had your coffee ready before you even made it back here. It's plain black coffee," I exclaimed.

Sammy shrugged. "I made a fresh pot. The other one was getting kind of old."

Most of our customers ordered lattes and cappuccinos, so it wasn't uncommon to find ourselves having to make a pot for just one customer.

Mike smiled. "Sammy takes care of me."

I almost pointed out that Sammy's job was to take care of the customers, but I was only tempted because I was a little annoyed at Mike wanting me to lay off my investigation. At the same time, I knew he was only doing his job, just like Sammy, so it didn't seem quite fair to snip at him about it.

Sammy handed the paper cup to Mike as the bell jingled to announce another customer coming through the door. "Gotta go!" She hurried off.

Mike winced as he took a sip of his coffee. "Hot!" he muttered. He shook his head a little bit then looked up at me. "So are we clear?"

I smiled and gave him a quick nod. "We're clear," I chirped.

We were perfectly clear—I fully understood that Mike didn't want me to continue investigating Joe's murder. Whether he understood that I was still going to do it, I didn't know.

"All right, then." He stood. "It was good to see you."

"You too," I replied genuinely. "Say hello to Sandra for me."

"I will." He tipped his coffee cup to me. "I'll see you around." He paused. "Well, as long as 'around' isn't Todd's Gym." He chuckled, and I wasn't sure if that was because he was confident that he wouldn't see me or that he would. "Enjoy your day!" Mike walked back out into the front of the café. "Bye, Sam," he called to Sammy.

"Bye, Mike," she replied, working over another customer's drink.

Relieved that my conversation with Mike was over, I turned back to my tea, trying to remember exactly what I had been doing when he'd interrupted me.

Chapter Ten

I had just picked up my teaspoon to measure out some tea for my testing when I heard another customer come in. I paused and listened to hear if Sammy would need me. She was speaking to someone, but I couldn't tell what she was saying. Then, she popped her head through the doorway.

"Someone's here to see you," she said.

"Who is it?" I wasn't expecting anyone and didn't know who might have been there that Sammy wouldn't have just sent back.

"You'll see," she said, a smile gracing her cherubic face. She disappeared from the doorway, apparently confident I would be following.

I put my teaspoon down among my piles of tea and headed out front.

There, looking nervous and proud, was Monica Basso, the namesake of Osteria di Monica. As always, she had her wire-rimmed glasses perched on her nose, and her kind blue eyes sparkled behind them. Though I had never seen it down, I knew her silvery-gray hair was rather long, based on the thickness of the bun she always had it wrapped in. She was wearing one of her standard floral-print dresses with modest high heels. I had no idea how she managed shoes like that at her age. I spotted a fairly substantial rolling cooler just behind her.

"Francesca!" she said excitedly, her face lighting up when she saw me.

"Monica!" Even though she was older than my mother had been, and my family was very strict about being respectful to my elders, I had always called her by her first name. I wasn't sure how that had come about or how I'd gotten away with it. "You came to see me?"

"Sì, Francesca, I did." Monica had been born in Italy and still occasionally lapsed into Italian here and there.

"What can I help you with?" I asked.

"Here, this is for you." She grasped the cooler by its handle and pulled it toward me.

"What is it?" I had an inkling of what it might have been but didn't want to get my hopes up too much, in case I was wrong.

"Tiramisu!" she declared.

I was right. "Really?" I squealed. A couple of customers glanced my way, but I didn't care. Maybe I could sell them some tiramisu! I knelt down and opened the cooler. It was full to the brim with neatly sliced pieces of tiramisu, each in an individual plastic container. By a quick count, I guessed there must have been about two dozen slices inside.

I looked up at Monica, a big grin on my face. "So you decided to do it?"

"Of course! Your grandmother and I talked about doing this years ago, and we never did. When Alberto told me you wanted to sell my tiramisu, how could I say no?"

I stood up and hugged her. "Oh, thank you so much. I'm so excited!"

Monica laughed good-naturedly. "There's no need to thank me, Francesca. You're the one selling my desserts!"

"But they're such good desserts. It's an honor to be able to sell them here." I caught Sammy eyeing the cooler from across the counter. I hadn't told her about my proposal to Alberto the night before, partly because I didn't expect Monica to be so quick to take me up on it. "Monica brought us some of her tiramisu to sell," I told her.

"Ohh," Sammy replied, drawing the word out. "Well, that's not going to be good for my waistline."

"Would you mind stocking the refrigerated display with these while I go talk to Monica in the back for a few minutes?" I pulled the cooler around to the back side of the counter for Sammy and then led Monica into the back room to work out the details of the agreement.

"So how much do you want to sell them for?" I asked. "The same price as the restaurant? More?"

"How about the same price? It's a fair price there. It's a fair price here."

"Okay, good." I smiled. "And how do you want to split the profits? I told Alberto we could do whatever you wanted."

"We'll split them evenly, of course," she replied.

"Are you sure? You're doing the hard work of making them. I'm just putting them in the case to sell."

"Evenly," she affirmed. "It's only fair."

I would have been happy to give her more money, but wasn't going to argue with her over it. I knew I'd never win. "Should we draw up a contract?" I asked, moving to sit down at the computer.

"Of course not!" Monica scoffed. "I don't need a contract with you."

"Are you sure?" I asked. I had lived in the big city long enough to expect to need a contract for any business deal. The small-town way of verbal agreements seemed foreign to me.

"A handshake," she replied firmly, "although I have known your family long enough to take you at your word."

She reached out her hand, and I took it.

"Thank you, Monica," I said.

"I already told you, I am the one grateful to you for giving me the opportunity to share my food with more people."

We went back out front, and Sammy wheeled the cooler around the counter for Monica to take with her.

"Should I bring more tomorrow?" Monica asked.

I nearly choked. "Tomorrow?" I looked over at the case, chock full of tiramisu. Our standard refrigerated offerings were relegated to a small section in one corner. I was grateful we had another case to store our other products in. As much as he loved Monica's tiramisu, Matt would have never forgiven me if I didn't have chocolate cupcakes on hand. I didn't see how we would possibly need another delivery of tiramisu the next day.

"Tomorrow's Friday," she said matter-of-factly as though that would make me understand. "I take the weekends off. I won't be able to bring you any more until Monday."

That made a little more sense, but I had asked Alberto for only five or ten pieces. I had no idea how long selling five would take, let alone twenty-five. I also worried about needing to throw some out if they didn't sell as well as I expected them to. I didn't want to have even more, that I might not be able to sell.

"Monica, I don't know if I can sell that many."

"Oh, don't worry, dear. I'm sure you will. And if you don't, you just take them home and give them to your friends and don't worry about paying me for them."

"Monica—" I started.

"I don't want to hear anything else about it! I'll see you tomorrow." She reached for the cooler, but Sammy swatted her hand away.

"I'll take it out for you," Sammy said. She and Monica headed out to Monica's car. I glanced around the café to make sure everyone was taken care of and then went into the back room to grab the chalkboards we used to advertise specials. One was small and counter-sized while the other was a full-size sandwich board for out front on the sidewalk. I laid the small one on the counter and took the other one out front. Monica was just pulling away from the curb. I handed Sammy a pack of multi-colored chalk.

"We've got some tiramisu to sell. Time for you to work your magic," I said.

Sammy had impeccable handwriting and impressive artistic skill. Whatever she would create would be way more visually appealing than whatever my efforts would produce. It wasn't just that I wanted to make sure we sold the tiramisu—I also had a compulsion to make sure everything I presented in relation to the café, from the drinks and food to the way it was decorated, was nice to look at.

"I'll do my best," she replied sunnily, taking the chalk. She slid out a blue piece and immediately started drawing on the large slate.

Before she had even finished writing the first word, I could tell the board was going to be beautiful. I left her to it and went inside to tend the counter, where I was surprised to see a customer waiting even though I'd only been outside for a minute.

"Can I help you?" I asked.

"Could I have a piece of tiramisu?" the woman asked. "It's my absolute favorite."

"Coming right up," I replied.

I removed the dessert from the container it had been delivered in and arranged it on a plate with a little paper doily before handing it to the woman, who was practically drooling by the time I put it in her hand. I could only hope that others would also be tempted by the tiramisu in the display.

Chapter Eleven

I couldn't believe how quickly we sold them. By the time Monica came with another, even bigger delivery the next day, we had almost completely sold through the first batch. I didn't know whether to credit Sammy's exquisitely drawn signs—complete with beautifully drawn slices of tiramisu—or the sheer deliciousness of Monica's desserts or downright luck, but I was astounded.

"I told you," Monica said when I told her. Her blue eyes were twinkling with pleasure behind her glasses.

"I just—I can't believe it!" I said. "I never dreamed we would sell that much. People bought multiples at a time."

"What can I say? People like good food," she replied.

I certainly had to agree. "Are you going to be able to keep up with making all the extras?" I asked, concerned that making twenty or more extra pieces of tiramisu a day would be too much for her. She wasn't as young as she used to be.

"Oh, sì, of course, Francesca. It's not difficult to make a little more for you. I just put out extra pans."

I laughed at what I knew was an over-simplification. My grandparents' attitude had been much the same, though—a little bit of extra cooking, baking, or whatever was no worry when one was already doing it. Even though I knew she had to multiply the recipe many times over, my grand-mother had always insisted that all she had to do to make an extra lasagna for the family down the street with the new baby or for the new teacher in town or for the widower who came into the café every day for a mozzarella-tomato-basil sandwich—or all three!—was to lay out an extra pan. I always wanted to point out that she still had to make the extra noodles and sauce and prepare the extra meat and cheese, but I knew she would have none of it. I had gotten the sense that the attitude of a little hospitality never being any trouble was something engrained in my grandparents and in Monica years before, back when they were in the old country.

"Well, I'm glad you're doing this, Monica," I said. "And I'm always sure to tell everyone who buys a slice about your restaurant."

"*Grazie mille*, Francesca. It's good for us to all work together."

I helped Monica load her coolers back into the car and set to work storing away the masses of tiramisu in my possession. Knowing that I had to make the second batch last through the weekend and that there wasn't any more room in the front display anyway, I stored some in the back room's refrigerator. I decided I would only put out a certain number each day, and when they were gone, they were gone. It was more important to me that we have some available every day than that we sell through them as quickly as possible. I wanted people to know that Antonia's had a steady stream of tiramisu coming in.

Satisfied that I had everything arranged satisfactorily, I went back out to the front. Sammy had taken the day off to go to the memorial service Joe's family was having for him, so I was working alongside Becky, one of the high schoolers who helped us out part-time. Her curly red hair was pulled and looped into a small ponytail at the back of her head, but fuzzy ringlets had escaped and were curled all around her face. I realized that constantly working over steaming-hot beverages wasn't the best way for her to keep her unruly locks in check.

She was preparing a drink for someone when another customer came in. She glanced up at the door.

"I got it," I said, crossing behind her toward the register. "Can I help you?" I asked the customer. He looked familiar, more familiar than one of the tourists who made multiple visits during their weeks of vacation but less familiar than a local. I struggled to place where I might know him from.

"I'd like a latte, please," he said in a thick Southern accent that just made me feel even more as though I knew him from somewhere.

"Anything else?"

"I'll take a piece of that tiramisu you got over there," he replied.

I was grateful Monica had brought so much to get us through the weekend. "You'll enjoy it. We just started carrying it. It's from a local restaurant called Osteria di Monica."

"If the tiramisu's good, I'll have to try that place out before I leave town."

"Oh, it is." I told him the price for the two items.

"It's busier in here than the last time I was in," he said as he handed me his credit card. "You got that shipment of tea all straightened out yet?"

I finally remembered who he was. He was the gentleman who had been in earlier in the week—the day Mrs. D'Angelo broke the news to Sammy, Matt, and me about Joe Davis's murder.

"I knew I recognized you!" I said with a smile. "I'm still working on the tea. I want to make sure I have my technique all sorted out before I put the new stuff on the menu. I'm hoping to have at least a couple tea drinks on the menu sometime next week."

I had pretty much come to the conclusion that I would never have time to sample the teas while I was at the café, so I'd taken the whole box home with me the night before and had spent the evening experimenting with different brewing temperatures and steeping times. I felt I had made pretty good progress.

"Well, I'll have to come back and try one," the man said.

"Are you in town that long?" I asked, somewhat surprised. Most people only spent a week in town before heading back to wherever they came from. I was certain the man had said he was just visiting, but maybe I'd misunderstood.

"I'm spending some time traveling all along the New England coast this summer," he said. "I'm sure I'll find myself back here soon enough."

"We'll look forward to seeing you. If you want to go grab a seat, I'll have this right out to you." I had been preparing his drink as we spoke and was ready to pour the milk into the espresso, a task I liked to be able to focus on. I also felt I had a reputation to live up to for that customer, especially since I seemed to remember having created a fairly intricate design in his foam the last time he was in.

I briefly considered pouring in a design based on a piece of tiramisu, but I had never practiced and wasn't sure it would come out as perfect as I wanted it. I decided on a self-referential design I usually only used for myself or Sammy when I was in a silly mood—a coffee cup with a few wisps of steam coming out, as though it contained its own fresh hot coffee. I poured the design in and held back a smile as I looked at the finished product. The man seemed the type that would appreciate the joke. I quickly arranged a piece of tiramisu on a plate and carried the drink and dessert over to the table where the man was seated.

"Here you go," I said, setting both dishes down so he could see my handiwork. To my delight, he chuckled when he saw the design in the latte.

"You definitely don't get a plain rosetta here, do you?" he laughed.

"Not if I'm working," I replied.

Sammy could hold her own with the standard designs, although she was better with a pen or a piece of chalk. Becky and the other kids who worked with us pretty much stuck with rosettas, leaves, and hearts.

"I'm Francesca, by the way," I said to him. "Or Fran. I'm the owner."

"It's a pleasure to meet you, Fran," he replied, reaching up to shake my hand. "I'm Jack." He paused and glanced around. "If you're Fran, I'm curious—who is Antonia? I assume you didn't just pick that name out of the blue."

"She was my grandmother. She and my grandfather opened this café almost seventy years ago after they moved here from Italy."

"And it's been in the family ever since?" he asked.

"It's been in the family ever since," I confirmed. "After my grandparents passed away, my mother took it over, and after she passed away earlier this summer, I took it on."

"I'm sorry to hear about your mother," he said, sounding surprisingly sincere for someone who had never known her. I guessed that was a by-product of his Southern charm.

"Thank you," I said. "The next time you come in, feel free to ask for me if I'm not out front. I'm not always here, but I am most afternoons."

"I'll do that," he said with a smile. "If only to see what design you'll come up with next."

"I'll take that as a challenge," I replied. As I walked away from his table, I told myself I'd have to spare some time from my tea experimentation to practice pouring a tiramisu design into a latte.

Chapter Twelve

Matt and I had planned to have dinner that night. As a way to avoid our constant debate over who was paying, he had offered to cook. It seemed to me a sneaky way to pay without being obvious about it, but I let it go. At least he was letting me bring the wine.

I arrived at his door a little while after closing up the café, a bottle of red in my hand and Latte at my feet. I was glad Matt didn't mind me bringing the pooch over. Thinking that he was all alone at my house while I was enjoying a pleasant meal just down the street would have made me sad.

As soon as Matt opened the door, tomato-stained wooden spoon in hand, the smell of Bolognese sauce poured out of the house, and my mouth started watering.

"It smells delicious, Matty," I exclaimed.

"Good," he replied with a smile, reaching out with his non-spoon-holding hand to hug me. "It should be ready in just a few minutes. I just have to throw the spaghetti in."

"Is there anything I can do to help?" I asked, stepping inside. Latte trotted past me and into the kitchen, where he knew Matt would have laid down a bowl of water and a rawhide for him.

"Open the wine."

We went back into the kitchen, and Matt handed me a corkscrew. It was one of the old-fashioned ones with no bells or whistles—just a twisted piece of metal that would shred a piece of cork if not used properly. Fortunately, I'd had some practice and was able to remove the cork in one try. Matt already had two wine glasses sitting on the table, so I poured the wine into them and sat down in one of the chairs.

"So how's everything going?" I asked. We hadn't seen each other since our dinner at

Osteria di Monica a few days earlier, and as quickly as new projects came up for him at work and old ones were put on hold, I figured he would have something new to tell me.

"Pretty good," he replied. "One of our big customers had an agreement fall through with a service provider yesterday, so we're scrambling to find them a new one. They're working on some really exciting stuff, and the other company chickened out, putting the whole project back to square one. Everything had been going really well with them, too."

I wasn't really sure what any of that meant, but it sounded important and mattered to Matt, so I did my best to follow along.

"Fortunately, we have plenty of contacts within the industry, so I don't think it'll take us long to find them a new partner. I actually think the new deal we're working on might turn out even better for them than the old one." Matt pulled a pan of garlic bread out of the oven and set it on a trivet next to the stove.

"Do you need help with that?" I asked.

"The project? I don't think you–"

"The garlic bread."

Matt laughed. "No, I got it. I was confused there for a minute about what contacts you had with Internet service providers. I guess you could have some from when you were in New York, though."

Actually, I did. However, they were all public-relations and marketing people—probably not the sort that could help him with his client's project.

Matt transferred the garlic bread to a plate and brought it to the table.

"Eat up," he said. "It's the best when it's still hot." To prove his point, he grabbed a piece off the top and shoved it in his mouth. "Careful, it's hot," he said around the bread he was holding delicately between his teeth to keep it from burning his lips.

"I think I'll wait a couple minutes," I said. "Might be safer."

"Suit yourself," he replied, but I noticed he still hadn't actually bitten into it.

I watched him as he moved around the kitchen for a few minutes, draining the spaghetti and mixing it with the sauce just enough to give it a good coating. He transferred the rest of the Bolognese into a bowl so we could each add however much we wanted to our individual plates.

"You know, you don't have to get all those dishes dirty," I said as he poured the spaghetti into another bowl to bring to the table. "I'm not above getting my food straight from the pot."

"What kind of host would I be if I did that?" he asked.

"Apparently the same kind I am," I retorted.

Matt laughed. "I'm just trying to make it nice for you. The meal's not fancy, so I may as well make the presentation look good."

I couldn't fault him for that, since it was a variation of my own approach to food.

He finally got everything ready and sat down across from me at the table. He took a long drink of his wine. "That's good wine," he announced. "I should have tried some earlier—I could have been on my second glass by now."

The wine was indeed really good. I'd been lucky enough to find it relatively inexpensively at a store nearby when they were cycling their inventory. I poured a little more into each of our glasses as Matt scooped spaghetti onto our plates.

"No sense in letting the glasses get low," I said with a smile.

"Did you just bring one bottle?"

"Yeah, but I have more at home."

"Good." Matt laughed. "I don't have to go to work tomorrow, so I don't have to hold back."

I laughed along with him as we dug into our meals. We had a long, rambling, pleasant conversation as we ate, one of those conversations where people talk about everything and nothing–his work, my work, TV shows we both liked, people from high school we both knew. I told him all about Monica's tiramisu and how well it was selling and gave him excruciating details about my experimentations with tea. The one thing we didn't talk about was the thing everybody else in town was talking about–Joe Davis's murder. It just didn't come up. Until I brought it up.

"I went to see Todd the other day," I said as Matt put the dishes in the dishwasher. I'd offered to do it and had even started, but he insisted on taking care of it, so I was leaning against the counter and sipping my wine as he worked.

He paused for a second, I thought, just before he asked, "You did, did you?"

"Yeah," I replied. "I really wanted to find out more about the murder and why the police suspected him."

"Hmm." He kept loading the dishwasher.

I wondered if I should tell him more about my visit to Todd.

"What did you find out?" he asked finally, saving me from needing to decide.

"They really don't have much on him," I said. "It's not even circumstantial. He was home alone watching TV. They think he must have done it just because it happened at his gym and he doesn't have an alibi."

"Or maybe they think he did it because he did it."

I looked at him in surprise. "You think he did it?"

Matt sighed. "I don't think he didn't do it."

"But why?"

"Because the police think he did it. Or he may have done it. They think it enough to investigate him. And because I'm not one of the cops investigating the case, I don't have the evidence that they have to know whether or not there's more that points to Todd. I don't assume blindly that he didn't do it because he doesn't *seem* like a murderer. Most murderers don't seem like murderers, Franny. That's how they manage to kill people. If everyone who was a murderer seemed like one, they wouldn't get the chance to murder anyone because no one would get near them."

I didn't know what to say. I didn't know where this was coming from. "I thought you were on my side," I said.

"I am on your side, Franny. I'm not on Todd's side."

I opened my mouth to protest, but Matt cut me off.

"I'm not against Todd either. Not unless he killed Joe. I'm against the murderer, whoever that is. Because I don't know who did it. And neither do you. Neither of us knows because neither of us were there and neither of us are the police."

"Matt, that's not fair," I managed to get out.

"What's not fair? That I won't let you keep going around, swearing up and down that Todd is innocent when you don't actually know? You haven't lived here since high school. You don't know how things have changed or what people have gotten into. You assume that Todd is the same guy you idolized back in high school, but you didn't even know him back then. Not really."

"No, Matt," I said angrily. "What's not fair is that you let me think that you were going to help me prove that Todd was innocent when this is how you really felt all along. You led me on. You let me think that we were a team. And you know what? I may not have known Todd that well back in high school, but I did know you pretty well, and I know you didn't like him. You didn't like anyone who was athletic, just because you weren't athletic. And now that we're all grown up, you're still carrying the same grudge. It's ridiculous, Matt! He's made a success of himself being an athlete, and you've made a success of yourself not being an athlete. It doesn't have to be one way or the other. Everyone can be happy doing what they're good at. Todd being a good athlete doesn't mean you can't be good at something else."

"Maybe you should tell him that, Franny. He's the one who's an arrogant jerk. He acts like he owns the world just because he has a big concrete block with his name on it. It's not that special. It's just a gym. I could go open one tomorrow that would be just as good as his because it's a *gym*. You put in some rooms with some mirrors, a few treadmills, some weights—boom! Matt's Gym! It's not that hard."

"You don't even go to the gym!" I shot back. "I have been to plenty of them, and plenty of them are not good. They have teachers who don't know what they're doing or machines that don't work right. It's not that easy. Todd has classes—good classes!—and lots of them. In Cape Bay, that's practically unheard of. It's a great gym—a beautiful place. Have you even been in there to see what it's like?"

"No," Matt admitted.

"See? You don't even know what it's like. How can you judge it if you've never been inside?"

Matt was quiet.

"You can judge it because Todd owns it—is that it?"

Matt still didn't say anything. He just leaned on the edge of the sink and stared out the window above it.

"That's it, isn't it?" I gave him a chance to answer, but he didn't. "Matt, you can't judge the place just because Todd owns it, and you can't hate Todd just because you did back in high school. It's not fair to him, and it doesn't do you any good either. How does it benefit you to dislike him so much? It doesn't. You need to let it go."

I was getting frustrated with Matt's continued silence. I didn't know whether he was doing it to make a point or to annoy me. Or maybe he'd just run out of things to say. I stared at the side of his head, trying to read what I could see of his expression. I got nothing. He didn't look angry or upset or sad or happy or any other emotion I could discern.

"Matt," I said finally.

He heaved a big sigh. "It seems like you've already made up your mind, Franny. I don't know if there's anything I can say at this point to convince you that Todd may have done it." I opened my mouth, but Matt, still staring out the window, held up his hand. "Not that he did it—just that he may have done it. Just that you should keep an open mind."

"He didn't even have a motive to kill him."

"You don't know that," he said.

"Is there something you know that you're not telling me?"

"No, Fran." He finally turned and looked at me. "Look, I know you've sat and talked with him and he's done nothing to raise your suspicions, but he wouldn't exactly come right out and announce it if he had a motive, would he? Especially not to the pretty girl from high school who just came back to town."

"Stop saying that Todd thinks I'm pretty. He doesn't, okay?"

"What makes you so sure?"

"I'm not a pretty, blond, perky, cheerleader type. I'm a calm, boring, normal-looking brunette. I'm not his type."

"Don't sell yourself short, Franny," he said quietly.

"We're not talking about me anyway, Matt. We're talking about you and why you dislike Todd so much."

"I thought we were talking about whether Todd killed Joe Davis."

"He didn't."

"You think."

"No, I know," I said firmly.

He looked at me, his warm brown eyes meeting my blue ones. I tried to keep my gaze strong and level, but I found that difficult when Matt was looking at me so intensely.

"Okay. You know." He paused and took a deep breath. "But I don't. I need some kind of evidence, some proof one way or the other. And until I get that, I can't say that I think Todd is innocent."

"Well, I do."

"That's fine," he said.

"And I'm going to keep looking for evidence that he didn't do it."

"Then I hope you won't fault me if I look for evidence that he did."

"You would work against me like that?" I asked, taken aback.

"It's not working against you, Franny. Wouldn't you rather have me look and find nothing than not look and find out later that there was something obvious that was missed because we weren't looking?"

"I would rather find the person who actually did it so I can prove it wasn't Todd."

"So would I. I would rather find out that it was someone I've never even seen before in my entire life. I don't want to think that anyone I know is capable of killing someone like that. But that doesn't mean I can just blindly rule out everyone I know."

I was at a loss for words. Part of me knew that Matt was right—that all leads had to be chased even when I didn't like where they went. But another part of me deeply believed that Todd wasn't a murderer and that to investigate him would be a waste of time—time that I could better spend finding the actual murderer.

"I understand how you feel," I said finally. And I did understand. I didn't agree, but I understood. Also, I wasn't going to be able to change his mind—at least, not until I had proof of Todd's innocence—so I decided I would drop the subject. For the time being.

Chapter Thirteen

Later that night, I sat on my couch with Latte curled up beside me, his head resting on my legs. I idly scratched him between the ears with one hand while I flipped TV channels with the other. A glass of wine sat on the end table next to me, waiting for my remote-control hand to be freed up. Unfortunately, it was late enough at night that there wasn't much interesting on except reruns of ancient sitcoms and talk shows aimed more at the drunk-college-student demographic than the wine-sipping over-thirty adult women.

By the time I'd made my way through all the channels, the hour had rolled over, and all the shows had changed. I couldn't stand the thought of going through all hundred-some channels again, so I switched over to the network whose lineup consisted primarily of shows that had originally aired when my mother was growing up and left it there.

I didn't actually care that much what I watched as long as my ears weren't ringing with the silence of the house. My mind was mostly occupied by my previous conversation with Matt. Or had it been an argument? Either way, that was what was on my mind.

I had been shocked by his reaction when I'd said the police didn't have much evidence against Todd. I recalled that he might have suggested that that was how he felt the other night, but I'd been focused on my own agenda and didn't notice it. Whatever the case, we clearly felt differently about whether or not Todd killed Joe. That was frustrating.

I actually wondered how much of Matt's doubt was rooted in high-school insecurities. He had been popular enough in the school newspaper–yearbook–band kid crowd we both ran in back then. He was always friendly and good-natured, and more than a few of my friends thought he was pretty cute. I had grown up side-by-side with him though, and he was more like a brother to me back then than anything else. Whenever my friends would comment on his looks, I stayed out of the conversation.

Matt was never scrawny or out of shape—he could always hold his own in gym class—but he wasn't an athlete like three-sport-letterman Todd. He always seemed to have a bit of an inferiority complex about that, too—as if being a trumpet player was somehow less worthwhile than being a football player. I never understood it. Todd particularly seemed to rouse Matt's ire for some reason. Matt calling Todd an arrogant jerk was nothing new—I'd heard variations of the sentiment since high school.

Part of what I never understood about it was that Todd was a great athlete, but Matt was a great student. He was so smart. He used to build circuits in his spare time, just for fun. He majored in electrical engineering, and not at an easy school either—he went to the best engineering school on the East Coast and graduated with a four-point-oh grade point average! And Todd owned a gym, sure, but Matt had an important job. He supervised people. He managed multimillion dollar projects. How was that less impressive than owning a gym?

Latte shoved his nose under my hand, and I realized I'd stopped petting him. I glanced at the clock. If I was going to get any sleep, I needed to take him out one last time and get to bed.

"Come on, boy," I said, unfolding myself from the couch. I walked to the front door and opened it for him. He darted out and ran around in the shadows. When he was finished, he ran back inside and straight up the steps to the second floor. He knew our routine. I followed him up to get ready for bed.

I lay in bed for a while after I woke up late the next morning. Latte was still asleep next to me, his head resting on the pillow as if he was a person. I loved when he did that. It cracked me up. We stayed that way for a few more minutes until my phone beeped, alerting me to a text message and waking up Latte. He rolled over onto his belly and looked around, trying to figure out what the noise was and where it had come from. He must have decided that, whatever it had been, it wasn't a threat, and laid his head down between his paws.

I rolled over and picked my phone up from the nightstand where I had it plugged in.

The text was from Matt. *Found something out about Joe. Want to meet for lunch?*

I thought for a minute about what Matt might have learned and whether it was something I would actually want to know. Ultimately, whether it was good news or bad news for Todd, I knew I needed to hear it and sooner rather than later. Delaying the inevitable wouldn't do anyone any good.

I texted Matt back. *Sure, 1 hr?*

One good thing about Matt living two houses down was that when we decided to go out and do something, we didn't have to go through the endless back-and-forth of "Where do you want to eat?" "I don't care—where do you want to eat?" "I could go anywhere, but Mexican sounds good." "Really? I was thinking sushi sounded good." Back in New York, with its thousands of restaurants, that conversation could take longer than the eventual meal. In Cape Bay with Matt though, we could hash that all out in person, which involved less typing and waiting.

Matt texted me back quickly. *Come over whenever you're ready.*

As soon as I got out of bed, Latte perked up, jumped off my bed, and pranced around the room, eager to get his breakfast and start the day. I laughed at his enthusiasm, wishing it was that easy for me to jump out of bed, raring to go. We made our way through our morning routine—breakfast for Latte, a quick shower and clean clothes for me—and then I took Latte on a walk around the block before giving him a treat to remember me by and heading down to Matt's house.

"Where do you want to eat?" Matt asked as we headed down the sidewalk toward Main Street.

One of the many things I loved about living in a small town was that we could just start heading toward the one street where everything was located and decide on the way where exactly we were going.

"I don't care—where do you want to eat?" I replied, holding up my end of the predictable conversation.

"I could really just go for a lobster roll and some fries," Matt said, giving voice to a craving I didn't even know I had until I heard him say it.

"Sandy's it is!" I said.

As we headed toward our favorite seafood joint, we avoided the two most obvious topics of conversation—Joe Davis's murder and our heated debate from the night before. We had ended the night on relatively good terms, agreeing to disagree, but there was still a little bit of tension between us. Instead, as we walked, we talked about the weather and how the summer tourist season was going. Even when we got to Sandy's, we talked about anything but Joe.

Even though I knew Matt had information I wanted—or needed—to hear, I was the one who had brought the case up the night before, which had ruined the evening, so I wasn't going to do it again. I would let Matt bring it up whenever he saw fit. Since whatever he'd found out about Joe was the whole pretext for our lunch, I knew he would get around to it sooner or later. I just had to bide my time even if I was incredibly impatient.

He finally brought it up after our food arrived.

"So, about Joe," he said just as I took a big bite of my lobster roll. I suspected he did it on purpose so I couldn't make much of a reply.

"Mm-hmm?" I mumbled through closed lips and a mouthful of buttery chopped lobster.

"I found out that he was three months behind on his gym-membership fees."

I swallowed my food and washed it down with a sip of my soda before responding. "So?" I asked.

"So, it's a possible point of contention between Joe and Todd."

I tried to keep from glaring at him. "I'm sure plenty of people are behind on their membership fees."

"Yes, but plenty of people aren't dead. Only Joe is."

"And so you think Todd killed him over three months of fees?"

"I didn't say that. I'm just telling you because it's a piece of information that I thought was relevant," he said calmly.

"And how did you get this piece of information?" I asked, his controlled demeanor only riling me up more. "Did you already know last night and just not mention it for some reason, or did you go out first thing in the morning to dig it up?" Both options annoyed me—that he'd been hiding something or that he was going out of his way to find information that could make Todd look bad.

"I didn't dig anything up. I woke up early this morning and went to the grocery store to pick up some stuff. While I was there, I ran into a guy I know who trained with Joe at Todd's Gym, and he told me that Joe was having money troubles and that he was behind on his gym dues. I figured it's something the police know, so I thought you'd want to know, too."

I studied his face carefully and ultimately chose to believe that he was being honest about his reasons for telling me. Matt had never been the type that would lie about anything, even things that seemed incon- sequential, so I had no reason to doubt him. Besides, he was right—if the police knew, I needed to know too. As much as I hated that he was right, I was glad at the same time. And even though I knew Matt thought the overdue gym fees were a potential motive for Todd, the fact that Joe was having money issues gave me another idea.

"You know, if Joe owed Todd money, I bet he owed other people money, too."

"It's possible." Matt picked up his lobster roll and took a bite out of it.

"I don't think it's just possible," I replied. "I think it's likely. I mean, how much are gym fees? Fifty dollars a month?"

"Probably a little more since he was doing his kickboxing training there and all."

I hadn't thought of that. That would have increased the cost. "Still," I said. "Even if it doubled the price, that's only three hundred dollars over three months. If money was that tight, he'd have to be cutting corners somewhere else, wouldn't he?"

"I guess so. Didn't Sammy say he had moved in with his parents?"

"Yeah, but that doesn't mean he didn't have other bills he may have been skimping on."

"True, but if you think not paying a bill is enough reason to kill someone, that doesn't rule Todd out."

"We're guessing that Joe only owed him about three hundred dollars, right?" I waited for Matt's response, which was just a nod. "That's not much off the bottom line," I finished.

Matt shrugged and picked up some fries. "Depends how tight his profit margins are." He pushed the fries into his mouth.

"Todd's Gym didn't look like the kind of place that was three hundred dollars away from shutting down." I took a bite of my own lobster roll while I waited for Matt to finish chewing and swallowing.

He had a lot of fries in his mouth, so it took him a minute. Finally, he said, "Looks can be deceiving. I've worked on projects with companies that were throwing cocktail parties right up until they closed their doors. Of course, I think some of those shut down *because* of the cocktail parties, but that's beside the point. The point is that you can't necessarily tell how strong a company's finances are by the way they look or act. Plenty of people would rather go down in a blaze of glory than let on beforehand that they were in trouble."

"I guess you're right," I conceded. "But if the gym was in that much trouble, why wouldn't Todd have told me that when I was talking to him?"

Matt looked at me with his eyebrows raised. He didn't even have to say anything. I knew what he was thinking.

"Because I'm a pretty girl?"

"Well, that, yeah. But it's also not like you guys have been close over the years. You just came back into town—have you even seen Todd in the past fifteen years?"

I shook my head.

"Not a lot of people are going to confess to someone they haven't seen in over a decade that their big, flashy business is in trouble."

Despite his subtle dig at Todd's Gym, I had to admit he had a point. "Could you stop being right? It's getting annoying."

Matt laughed, covering his mouth to keep from spitting half-chewed lobster all over the table. That in turn made me laugh, and just like that, all the tension between us was gone.

"I'll try," Matt said. "But I've had a lot of practice at it, so it'll be a hard habit to break."

I giggled again and took another sip of my soda. "You're too much, Matty."

"Ah, you like it."

I did like it, and I was surprised to realize I was going to miss him when he was out of town the next week. Since we'd reconnected, we'd seen each other almost every day, if only because we lived so close. But I knew what I was going to do with the time that he was away. I was going to go talk to Todd again and see if I could find out the state of the gym's finances and whether Joe's three months of delinquent payments could really be hurting them—or, at the very least, see if I could tell whether he was hiding anything from me.

Chapter Fourteen

After lunch on Saturday, Matt had some work stuff to take care of before he left for Virginia, so we walked back to our street. Matt went to his house to hole up with his laptop and send a million or so e-mails so everyone would know who was responsible for which aspect of what project. I didn't have to be at the café until late afternoon, so I went down to my house to get Latte and go for a walk.

He bounced around on the end of his bright-blue leash as we walked back in the direction I had just come from with Matt. I felt like going down to the beach even though I knew it would be packed with families of tourists. I just wanted to walk down the boardwalk and listen to the sound of the waves even if they were punctuated by the shouts of playing children.

The beach was packed, since all the timeshares and rentals turned over on Saturdays. Everyone wanted to get one last day on the sand before they headed home. Mother Nature had kindly given them a beautiful, sunny day by which to remember Cape Bay, and it seemed that almost no one had decided to stay in.

Latte was popular on the boardwalk, and he loved the attention he got from all the dog lovers. We could barely walk five feet without someone stopping to pet him or a toddler pointing out the "doggie woof woof." The walk wasn't exactly relaxing, but at least it served to get my mind off of Joe Davis's murder.

When we'd walked the entire length of the boardwalk, we turned around and made our way back the way we'd come, again stopped by excited tourists, some of whom had just seen us on our way down the beach. Even though it was on the hot side of warm out, I didn't quite feel like going home yet, so we took the long way, making our way through town to the park. The typical gaggle of old men was collected around the concrete chess tables, ostensibly competing, but more likely spending most of their time socializing.

We gradually made our way across the park and down a set of stairs that led to a pond. I noticed a crumpled piece of paper in the corner of one of the steps. Annoyed with whatever litterbug had left it there, I picked up the garbage and carried it to the nearest trash can. We continued through the back of the park and onto my street. When we got to the sidewalk in front of my house, I let Latte off his leash. I pulled out the tennis ball that I'd shoved in my pocket on the way out of the house and threw it as far as I could down the side of the house and into the backyard.

The backyards all along our street were nice and deep, with a natural fence along the back formed by a row of hedges and a thicket of trees. If I stood at the front of the yard and threw as hard as I could, Latte could get a good run in on the way to the ball and back. I threw the ball and let him chase it several times until he eventually let me know he had had enough exercise by lying down at my feet with the tennis ball in his mouth instead of dropping it as he did when he wanted to keep playing.

"Okay," I said, leaning down and holding out my hand for him to drop the drool-covered tennis ball into it. I held it gingerly between my thumb and forefinger, trying to get as little dog slobber on my hands as possible. Latte waited patiently as I unlocked the front door, but I could tell he was ready to get inside, get a drink of water, and relax on my bed in the air conditioning. I, meanwhile, had to change and get to work.

When I arrived, the café was completely slammed. Becky was working the register, calling out one drink after the next for Sammy to prepare. Sammy was making multiple drinks at a time, expertly pulling espresso and steaming milk in quick succession to prepare each customer's order. Becky herself handled the orders of food or plain coffee, quickly grabbing each component and passing them to the customer before taking the next order.

I grabbed my apron off its hook and slid it over my head. "I got the next one," I called as I tied the strings behind my back. I saw Sammy glance up in relief as Becky called out the next order.

"One cappuccino, one latte, one mocha," she announced.

"One cappuccino, one latte, one mocha," I confirmed as I lined up the cups and started the espresso.

"I also asked for two cupcakes and a cup of black coffee," the woman on the other side of the register said huffily.

"Yes, ma'am, I'm getting those now," Becky replied as she darted behind me and Sammy to the coffee pot. I was impressed with how well she handled the woman's rudeness, letting it roll off her back as though it was nothing. I wasn't sure I would have been that composed about it back when I was her age. I probably would have gotten anxious and wondered what I had done wrong.

Becky handed the woman the plain coffee and two cupcakes. "We'll bring the other drinks over to you as soon as they're ready," she said with a smile. She looked over the woman's shoulder at the next customer. "May I help you, sir?" she asked.

The woman reluctantly stepped aside, seeming annoyed that she hadn't managed to fluster Becky. She stood across the espresso machine from me, craning her neck to try to see what I was doing. I flashed her a smile and kept working. I knew I didn't have the time to linger over something intricate and I didn't particularly want to give any ammunition to the demanding woman staring me down, so I poured in designs that were quick but beautiful—swans encircled by hearts, tulips beside rosettas, a spiral of hearts.

Sammy came back from delivering a tray of drinks just as Becky called out the next order.

"Two lattes!"

"Two lattes!" Sammy echoed. She grabbed two cups and saucers and started preparing the drinks.

I looked up at the woman in front of me. "If you'd like to take a seat, I'll bring these over to you." I carefully arranged the three cups on a tray.

"All the tables are taken," she huffed.

"I think there are some chairs open in the corner," I replied, keeping the smile on my face. "Or there are a couple of tables outside."

The woman made annoyed little noises as she glanced around the coffee shop. I didn't know what she wanted me to do—she was already holding a cup of coffee and two cupcakes in her hands. There was no way she could hold more. And with an order of four coffees, I knew she had to be there with other people who must be somewhere nearby. She either finally spotted them or finally decided I didn't require any further supervision because she tromped off across the café to a table with three people and an empty chair just as I picked up the tray.

I walked over and dropped off the drinks, making it a point to smile brightly as I did so. My grandparents never would have tolerated me being anything but unfailingly polite to a customer, no matter how abrasive she was. I made it back to the counter just as Becky called out the next order.

We continued like that for the next hour or so until the traffic in the café died down.

"Why didn't you call me to come in?" I asked Sammy as we wiped all traces of the rush from the counters. Becky was busy gathering up dishes left on the tables and carrying them back to be washed.

"It just got busy all of a sudden. Everything was calm and quiet, and then it was like somebody rang a bell or something, and the whole beach decided to come in. You know how it is when it's a nice day and then it starts pouring rain and everyone runs in from the beach? It was like that, except with not a cloud in the sky."

"Well, you know you can call me in if I'm not here, anytime you need me."

"Of course," she replied.

We worked on cleaning up for a few more minutes until Becky finished clearing the dishes and disappeared into the back to wash them. It wasn't that I didn't want her to hear what I wanted to ask Sammy, but I wanted to be sensitive to Sammy's feelings.

"How was Joe's funeral?" I asked.

She sighed. "It was rough," she said. "You know, he'd had such a hard time lately, but it seemed like he was finally getting back on his feet. Or at least getting his act together. I didn't know this, but his parents were paying for him to take some computer classes at the community college so he'd have better skills to get a job." She sniffed and grabbed a napkin from her counter to dab her eyes. "Melissa was there with Emmy—that was really hard."

"Who are Melissa and Emmy?" I asked, thinking Joe perhaps had younger sisters or they were friends of Sammy who had been close to Joe.

"Melissa is his ex-girlfriend. And Emmy is their daughter."

"Oh." That was the only thing I could think to say. Among all the people I'd talked to about Joe, no one had ever mentioned a daughter. I wondered if she was something he kept quiet. "I had no idea."

"It's weird, but somehow it made it worse that you could tell Emmy had no idea what was going on. She was sitting up there in the front row with Melissa and Joe's parents, and every few minutes, she'd turn around to make faces at everyone. Melissa had to keep sitting her back down and telling her to be quiet, but it was like she could see how sad everyone was and just wanted to cheer them up. Gosh, Joe was so proud of her, too. He'd show me pictures every time he came in and just go on and on about all the new things she was doing."

So much for the secret-child thing. Still, I wondered if that might be a lead. If the spouse was always the first suspect when someone was murdered, didn't it stand to reason that the ex-girlfriend and mother of the victim's child would be a prime suspect?

"It just killed him that he couldn't pay child support after he lost his job." Sammy's eyes got big, and her hand flew to her mouth when she realized what she'd said. "Oh! I didn't... I didn't mean−" She grabbed another napkin and held it to her face. I reached out my hand and rubbed her shoulder.

"It's okay. I know it's just an expression."

"An awful expression!"

"Unfortunate," I said.

I hesitated, wanting to ask her something, but I didn't know how to phrase it without sounding as though I was suggesting, well, exactly what I was suggesting. In the end, I decided to just go for it. "Sammy, you don't think Melissa..." I trailed off and let her fill in the rest of the sentence.

She took a few seconds to put together what I was asking, but understanding finally appeared on her face. "Oh my gosh, no! Melissa would never... No! No, I can't even imagine. Melissa wouldn't do that."

"Okay," I said quickly, ready to move the conversation in a different direction. If Sammy didn't think Melissa could have done it, I wasn't going to push her. "I'm just grasping at straws. It's creepy knowing there's a murderer on the loose."

"I know," Sammy sniffled. "It's so scary thinking that it might have been random. Is there someone out there just looking for people walking alone to stab?" She shuddered. "I don't even like to think about it."

I thought her statement might have been inspired by more than just idle fear. "Are you worried that something might happen to you coming to and from here?" It was getting dark early enough that whether Sammy opened or closed the café, she was walking in the dark. Even if she drove in, she'd still have to come in from the parking lot on her own, and a parking lot was where Joe was murdered.

Sammy hesitated, but I could see the look on her face and guess what was coming. "I know it's stupid, but–"

"It's not stupid," I said, interrupting her. I looked at Becky in the back room. She was only sixteen and just a little tiny wisp of a thing. She and the other part-timers normally worked during daylight hours, just because that's when we needed the most help, but occasionally they helped open or close. I would feel awful if anything happened to them. "I'll call Mike and see if he knows anybody who could help make sure you get to and from work safely."

A big smile came across her face. "Thanks, Fran. Like I said, I feel silly, but I just keep waiting for some guy to come out of the shadows and get me."

"Don't worry about it," I replied. "I don't know what Mike will say or how long it will take to get something figured out, but I want you guys to be safe. But that reminds me—isn't it time for you to go home? You've been here all day."

Sammy glanced at the big wrought-iron clock on the wall. "Yeah, I guess it is time for me to get out of here." She slung the rag she'd been wiping the counters with over her shoulder. "I guess I'll see you tomorrow?"

"Yup, see you tomorrow."

Sammy went in the back, took her apron off, and dropped her rag in the basket we had for laundry. She grabbed her purse and turned around to wave to Becky and me. "Bye, guys!"

I waved and said goodbye, and Becky lifted a soapy gloved hand in Sammy's direction. I walked over to the door to the back room.

"What time did you come in?" I asked Becky.

"Noon."

"Why don't you head home when you're done?" I was putting myself at risk if things got busy again, but she'd already worked plenty of hours, and my talk with Sammy had me thinking it was best for her to get home before dark.

"Okay, cool!" She smiled, so excited that I got the feeling she had plans for the evening.

I went back out to the front to finish cleaning up the few remaining signs of our hectic hour. Everything was neat and orderly by the time Becky stuck her head out from the back.

"I'm all finished. Are you sure there isn't anything else you want me to do before I go?"

"Nope. Go. Enjoy your Saturday night."

"Awesome, thank you!" She was so happy she was practically jumping up and down. She pulled off her apron, hung it on the hook, and then disappeared out the back door so quickly I thought she was worried I would change my mind if she waited another second.

I checked behind her to make sure the back door was closed and locked, and I crossed my fingers and hoped we wouldn't have another wave of customers.

Chapter Fifteen

A slow but steady stream of people came in, keeping me busy enough that I wasn't bored but not so busy that things got out of hand. It was getting close to closing time, and only a couple of customers were left sitting and chatting in the big armchairs when the bell over the door jingled and I looked up to see Todd.

"Hi," I said cheerfully. I liked seeing a friendly face after a fairly busy day, and I had questions to ask him anyway.

"Hi, yourself," he replied. He glanced around the café as he walked up to the counter, where I was standing. "I thought you said the roses I sent you were still alive.

Or did you take them home to enjoy them there?"

"They finally died," I said. "I actually just threw them out yesterday." They'd lived a good life, and I probably would have kept them a little longer if I actually had taken them home, but I didn't think wilting flowers really made customers feel as though we were a clean, well-run establishment. "They were beautiful while they lasted, though," I assured him.

"Well, I guess I'll just have to see about getting you some new ones, then," he said and winked at me. I didn't know what to make of the wink, so I ignored it.

"I actually did want to know what florist you got them from. They were so beautiful and they lasted for so long, I was thinking it might be nice to have them in the café more often."

"Are you trying to tell me that you don't want me to send you more flowers?" he asked, leaning across the counter toward me.

"Well, I don't want you to feel like you're responsible for making sure we always have fresh ones!" I laughed, avoiding the question I knew he was actually asking.

He chuckled and ran his fingers through his thick blond hair, almost as if he was deliberately trying to draw my attention to it.

"So can I get you anything?" I asked.

"I would love one of your amazing lattes."

"Coming right up." I started preparing his drink. "Can I get you anything else? Something to eat, maybe?"

He leaned back to look at the display case with its assortment of heavy, rich baked goods and shook his head. "Nah, it's not my cheat day. The latte will already be more than I should have."

I always thought of cheat days as being associated with diet-conscious fashionistas, but I understood how that approach to eating could be something they shared with athletic, exercise-junkie types like Todd. Somehow, I thought Todd's cheat-day foods were more substantial than the cocktails the girls in New York splurged on.

I finished pouring a daisy into Todd's coffee and started working on one for myself. "Do you mind if I join you for just a minute?" I asked. "I had something I wanted to ask you about."

"Not at all," he replied, his broad smile revealing his gleaming white teeth.

"Let me just make my drink real quick, and I'll bring them around." I saw him reach for his wallet. "You don't owe me anything," I said, waving him off. "It's on the house."

He smiled that brilliant smile at me. "Thanks, Franny."

He went and sat down at one of the tables while I finished preparing my drink. I poured a many-leaved tulip into my cup and then took both drinks over to the table. I set Todd's down carefully in front of him so the daisy was facing the right way, and I took the seat opposite him, angling my chair so I could see any customers walking in or out of the door.

"So you said you wanted to talk to me?" Todd leaned toward me across the table.

"Yeah," I said distractedly as I watched to make sure a customer walking toward the counter didn't need me for anything. When she turned around after grabbing a napkin, I directed my attention back to Todd. "I wanted to ask you something about Joe."

"Oh." Todd leaned back in his chair. He sighed. "What do you want to know?"

"Well, I heard that Joe was three months behind in his membership dues."

His eyes narrowed. "Where did you hear that?"

"It doesn't matter where I heard it–" I started to say before Todd cut me off.

"No, I want to know. If someone's sharing confidential information about my members, I want to know."

I sighed. "I heard it from Matt. But he heard it from someone who trained with Joe at the gym. It wasn't a staff member or anything like that."

"Are you sure?"

"I'm as sure as I can be. I don't think Matt would go to the trouble of making up something like that."

"Okay." Todd crossed his arms against his muscular chest.

"So I take it it's true? Joe was behind on his dues?"

"Yeah."

"Was that something that concerned you?"

"You mean was I worried about him not being able to pay or was I worried about missing out on the money?"

"Either," I replied. "Both."

"Yeah, I mean, I was worried about him being out of work and living with his parents, but I wasn't worried about the money. One guy's not going to break me."

"You weren't worried about setting a precedent or anything?"

He looked at me curiously. "No."

"Why'd you let him get away with it? Not paying and still coming to the gym, I mean. Why'd you let him work out if he wasn't paying you?"

"You ask a lot of questions."

"I'm trying to help you, Todd," I replied. "When Matt came to me and told me about how far behind Joe was, he thought it was a possible motive. If I'm going to help you, I need to know why you let him keep working out."

"He still doesn't like me, huh?" He scoffed.

"Who?" I asked. "Matt?" I hesitated, searching for the best thing to say. I was surprised Todd knew of Matt's distaste for him, although I realized at the same time that I shouldn't have been. They'd lived in the same small town for most of their lives. Of course Todd would have noticed Matt didn't like him. "No, when he told me, it was for the same reason I'm asking you now—so we could eliminate it as a possibility. We need to rule everything out so we know when we find the real murderer and the real motive. If we have two people with two good motives, it doesn't help us. Especially not if one of those people is you."

Todd clenched his jaw a couple times, apparently thinking over what I had said. Finally, he gave in. "He was my friend. And he was having a hard time. I'm not going to screw over my friend just because he's having a hard time. Especially not when I don't need the money. Besides, kickboxing was Joe's way out. If I took that away from him, he'd be stuck in his parents' house forever."

"Hmm," I murmured. I took a sip of my coffee as I mulled over what Todd had said. I believed him, of course, about not being concerned about Joe's debt because he was a friend. He said it far too casually for it to be a cover-up of some sort. I was more perplexed by Todd saying that kickboxing was Joe's only road to get his life back in order. I knew he'd said before that Joe had promise, but he'd also said Joe was getting too old to be coming up in the sport and he didn't have the skills that some of the other guys had. I hadn't taken that to mean that he had a promising future in the sport. But Todd was talking about how kickboxing was Joe's only hope. And that, after Sammy had told me that Joe had been taking night classes to help him get a job.

"When I talked to you the other day, I thought you made it sound like he wasn't good enough to make a living off of kickboxing," I said finally.

"Did I?"

I waited for him to go on, but he didn't. "Yes, you did."

He shrugged and shook his head the slightest bit. "It's been a crazy week. I can't remember what I say from one day to the next."

"Oh well." I decided to laugh it off. It wasn't going to do any good to press Todd on which he really meant. Either he had been telling the truth then and being generous to the memory of a dead man now, or something, possibly grief, had led him to undersell Joe's skill when he first talked to me. I didn't think I was going to get him to admit to either option.

However, I was a little surprised that Todd thought the best way for Joe—a young out-of-work father rapidly coming up on thirty—to make a living was to literally fight for it. A nice, calm office job seemed like a much better—and safer—bet to me.

It was getting close to closing time when we finished our coffee. The other customers had gone, and no one else had come in, so it was just the two of us in the café when I picked up our cups and saucers to take to the sink in the back. Mine was light, but his was heavy. I glanced down and saw he'd taken maybe one sip as the daisy I'd crafted with the milk was barely distorted. I had to admit I was a little disappointed he hadn't drunk any more of it, but I was even more worried that something had been wrong with it.

"Was there something wrong with the coffee?"

"What?" Todd looked up from his phone, which he'd pulled out of his pocket.

"The coffee. Was there something wrong with it? You hardly drank any of it."

"Oh. No. Just gotta watch what I eat," he said.

When paying customers said stuff like that, I usually just shrugged it off. I didn't understand why people would come in and pay good money for drinks they weren't actually going to consume, but as far as I'm concerned, the customer is always right, so I didn't let it bother me.

Somehow though, Todd's full cup did bother me because I'd given the drink away for free—almost as though I had given him a gift and he'd shrugged, said "Oh, that's nice," and never looked at it again.

I tried to push that out of my mind, though. As Todd had said, he'd had a crazy week, and I would be nuts to take it personally.

I had a few dishes to wash and a little bit of cleaning up to do before I could head out for the night. With Sammy's worries about the safety of walking home alone in the dark ringing in my ears, I thought I would ask Todd if he could wait a few minutes and then walk me home or, I supposed, drive me if he'd brought his car.

I had just deposited the dirty dishes in the sink when I heard his voice behind me.

"Hey, Franny?"

I turned around to see him leaning into the doorway, his hands pressed into either side of the doorway, his cell phone clutched between his fingers.

"Yeah?" I asked.

"I'm going to get out of here, okay?"

"I was actually just about to ask if you could hang out for a few minutes until I get everything ready to lock up and then walk me home."

A look I couldn't quite define passed over his face, and for a second I thought he was going to agree. "I can't," he said. "I have to meet someone. You'll be okay getting home on your own?"

"Yeah, I'll be fine," I assured him. "Go. Don't let me keep you."

"Cool. Thanks for the coffee." He stepped all the way into the room and wrapped his arms around me in a quick hug. "I'll see you soon, a'right?"

"Okay," I said.

He strode across the café and out the door, setting the bell jingling as he flung it open.

I glanced at the clock, then went behind him and turned the lock in the door. As I walked back to take care of the dishes, I pulled my phone out of my pocket and sent Matt a text. *Any way you can spare a few minutes to come walk me home? Murder has me spooked.*

He texted me back shortly. *Sure thing. I'll be there in a few.*

I felt silly asking him to escort me like that, but I was glad I could rely on him.

I washed the few dirty dishes and was wiping down the tables when I heard a rap on the glass door. I almost jumped out of my skin, but when I looked, it was only Matt.

"I didn't mean to scare you like that," he said when I opened the door.

"It was that obvious?"

"You jumped about a mile high." He laughed. "I thought about just standing outside until you noticed me so I wouldn't startle you, but I thought that might be scarier."

"Please, do not ever do that. I would have a heart attack. You would have to break through the glass to come rescue me."

"I'd do it," he replied.

"Scare me like that or rescue me?"

"Rescue you. I don't want to have to do it, so I'll try not to ever scare you that bad."

"Thanks," I said. "But if you could try not to scare me at all, that would be even better."

Matt laughed. "I'll do my best." He looked around the café. "Are you ready to go, or is there something I can help you with?"

"I just have to wipe down the last of these tables, and then I'll be ready," I said. "Do you want a cup of coffee or anything?"

Matt wandered over to the display case. "No, no coffee," he said, peering inside. "I'd ask for a piece of tiramisu, but that might be hard to eat. Can I have a cupcake?"

"Chocolate?"

"Of course!"

"Help yourself." I ran my cloth over the last of the tables. Satisfied everything was cleaned to my standards, I headed for the back room to take off my apron and grab my purse.

"Oh my God, Franny." Matt groaned.

"Good?" I asked, poking my head out and seeing him go for a second bite of cupcake.

"I think it's the best you've ever made."

"You say that about everything I make."

"Then stop making such good food."

I laughed at him as I slid my purse over my shoulder. "Are you ready to go? Can you manage to eat and walk at the same time?"

"I'll try," he said. "If it turns out I can't, we can sit down on the curb until I'm done."

I laughed again. "Let's go," I said, shepherding him out the door and locking it behind us. "You can hold onto my elbow if you have to."

Matt chuckled, barely managing to keep the cupcake in his mouth, and we headed down the street toward home.

Chapter Sixteen

"Todd came into the café today," I said as we walked down the street.

Matt cocked his eyebrow at me but didn't say anything because his mouth was full of cupcake.

"I was going to ask him to walk me home, but he had to leave."

"Oh, so I was your second choice?" Matt asked after swallowing the bite he had in his mouth.

I looked up to study his face in the streetlight, but I couldn't quite tell whether he was just giving me a hard time. "I just knew you were working and didn't want to make you come all the way out when he was already there."

"I don't mind walking you home, especially if you don't feel safe walking alone."

"I know, I just—he was there. It made sense."

"He's a suspect in a murder case, Franny."

"That doesn't mean he's a murderer."

Matt gave me a "we've talked about this" look, so I knew Todd's innocence wasn't worth trying to go over any more.

"Anyway, while he was there, I asked him about Joe being behind in his dues."

"And?" he asked as he took another bite of his cupcake. He was practically inhaling it and only had a couple bites left. And it was not a small cupcake.

"And he says that he didn't care because Joe was his friend."

Matt almost spat the chocolate confection from his mouth. "I don't believe that," he said.

"What? Why not?"

"I just don't buy it." He shrugged.

"Tell me why. Do you not believe Todd would give his friend a pass on his dues? Or do you not think Todd could possibly have any friends?"

"I just don't think he's that generous."

"Because you don't like him."

"I didn't say that," he replied, shoving the last piece of cupcake in his mouth.

"You didn't have to."

We walked on quietly. I was feeling conflicted. I believed Todd, but Matt was my good friend and maybe more. However, that "maybe more" seemed to have gotten sidetracked with the news of Joe's murder. I think it was bothering both of us more than we liked to admit–Matt because it reminded him of his dad's murder and me because, well, why *wouldn't* a murder in my small hometown bother me? Whatever the exact reasons, I felt like we'd both been distracted the past few days.

"It's not that I don't like him," Matt said after a few minutes. "I just don't get why the guy would charge his friend for membership in the first place but not care that he can't pay. Why not just let your friend work out for free in the first place?"

"Maybe because all his friends would think they should get to work out for free and then he wouldn't make any money?"

"You give me free cupcakes."

"Yeah, but you don't come in *expecting* free cupcakes. You always offer to pay."

"I only do that to make you *think* I don't expect free cupcakes. I always expect free cupcakes. Free cupcakes, free coffee, free tiramisu. I expect it all to be free."

I looked over at him to see if he was serious. The twinkle in his eye and the upturned corner of his mouth told me he wasn't.

"My point is," I said, rolling my eyes, "that it makes sense to me he would charge everyone as a rule but give his friend a break when he needed it."

"I don't know. I just don't buy it. I just don't think you let people get away with not paying you the money you need to run a business."

"I don't think he's hurting for it."

"Why? Did you ask him about that too?"

"No. It was just the way he talked about it. Like he was really doing Joe a favor. Because he cared about him and he wanted to."

Matt give me a sidelong glance, which I chose to ignore. "You're too nice, you know that, Franny?"

"Yeah, I know. That's why I keep hanging out with you."

Matt looked at me curiously and then burst out laughing. "I guess I had that one coming, huh?"

"Yup, you did."

We walked along a little further then in a more comfortable silence.

"So should I plan to walk you home every night until Joe's killer is caught?" Matt asked as we walked up to my house.

"You could, but you leave for Virginia tomorrow, don't you? Might make it a little difficult."

"Oh, that's right!" Matt groaned. "I forgot about that. I guess I won't be doing the honors then, will I?"

"Guess not." I shrugged.

"You're not going to ask Todd to walk you home every night, are you?"

I thought about teasing him and saying yes, but I decided to go easy on him. "No, I actually promised Sammy I'd call Mike and see if he knows someone who could provide an escort. It's not so much that I'm worried about me walking alone as that I'd never be able to forgive myself if something happened to Sammy or Becky or any of the other girls. It's dark now when we open and when we close."

"Hard to believe it's that time of year already."

"I know. The season's flown by. It's hard to believe it's almost over."

"It's been a crazy summer."

"You can say that again," I agreed as I slid my key into the lock. Latte bolted down the stairs as soon as the sound reached his ears. I opened the door, and he flew out into the yard, running around Matt and me and shoving his wet nose into our hands.

"Looks like somebody's happy to see you," Matt said.

"Yeah, it's nice having somebody so excited to see me when I get home every day."

"Hey, maybe I should get a dog."

"You should. Latte could have a little friend to play with." Latte raced past us as I spoke and went straight back into the kitchen. I knew he would be sitting by his bowl with his little paw up in the air, waiting patiently for me to serve him his dinner. "Guess I better go take care of him," I said.

"Yeah, I should get home—I still have some stuff to take care of before I leave tomorrow."

"Will I see you before you leave, or should I say goodbye now?"

"You can always say goodbye now and then again tomorrow if we see each other."

I stepped toward him and put my arms up around his neck. "Have a safe trip, okay?"

"I'll try," he said, his arms wrapped around my back.

"Don't try," I admonished playfully. "Just do it."

"Yes, ma'am." He chuckled as he stepped off my front step. "If I don't see you tomorrow, I'll see you in a couple of days."

"Okay, see you then. Good night." I gave him a little wave as I stepped inside.

"'Night, Franny."

I shut the door and went to feed Latte, who was, as I'd predicted, patiently waiting for his supper. I fed him and let him out again and then headed upstairs to go to bed. It was early, but I was tired. As soon as

I climbed into bed, Latte hopped up next to me, snuggling in close. I ran my fingers through his fur as I waited for sleep to come. It did not. Despite how tired I was, my mind was racing.

I thought about Matt and Todd and Joe and Melissa. I wanted to talk to Melissa, but I didn't know her last name or where she lived or anything about her except that she was Joe's ex-girlfriend and they had a daughter named Emmy. That was nothing—nowhere near enough information to find her. I couldn't even look her up online with that much information. Though Cape Bay was small, I figured at least ten or twenty Melissas lived there, and even if I could find them all, I didn't think they'd appreciate me showing up to talk to them.

I tried to think of some other way to track her down and realized I could always ask Sammy—I could tell her I wanted to send a sympathy card. But that would be dishonest, and I didn't want to deceive a friend like that. There was Mrs. D'Angelo. She knew everything about everyone in town. I was sure she didn't approve of Joe and Melissa having a baby without being married, but I didn't see why that would stop her from giving me some more information about Melissa.

That was the last thought I remembered before waking up to the sun shining in my face and Latte staring at me.

"Good morning," I told him. He gave me a good lick, running his tongue from my chin to my forehead. I pulled the sheet up to wipe away his slobber and gave his head a good scratch. "Should we go play in the park today?"

I didn't know how he could possibly understand me, but he jumped to his feet and stared at me, his tongue out, panting excitedly, the exact same way he did when we played fetch.

"I'll take that as a yes," I said. I got out of bed and went about getting both of us ready for a trip to the park.

Less than an hour later, we were in the park, getting ready for an intense game of fetch. We went to a corner of the park I didn't often go to, where there was a playground and a couple of fenced-in fields the rec leagues and kids in general used to play soccer or baseball.

A dog park was in the works for Cape Bay, but we didn't yet have one. We'd actually only gotten a leash law in the past five years or so. It had just never been an issue. People would go to the park to let their dogs run around and have fun without any issues. But someone had moved to town from somewhere that did have leash laws and had complained so vociferously about the lack of regulation that the town had no choice but to start requiring everyone to keep their dogs on leashes, even in the park.

Long-time residents then complained that there was nowhere for their dogs to run free, which led to the development of the dog park. It was supposed to have been built in the next year or so, but until then, residents had begun using the playing fields as a de facto dog park—they were fenced in, they had a gate, they had enough space for a dog to run, so they were perfect.

We had been playing fetch for several minutes when, instead of returning the ball to me, Latte shot past me with the ball and made a beeline for the gate.

"Latte, come here!" I called out, turning around to see what he was trying to get to. I hadn't realized that anyone had arrived to play at the playground, but Latte clearly had, and he apparently wanted them to join our game. A small child and a woman I assumed to be the child's mother were sitting on a bench keeping watch. The child had caught sight of Latte and was walking across the mulched playground toward the fields. Latte ran right up to the fence and dropped his ball in the gap between the gate and the fence. He lowered his nose to the ground and nudged the ball through.

The child at the playground seemed to understand Latte's invitation and took off running toward us. I couldn't quite tell, based on the child's chin-length brown hair or plain blue-and-white shorts and T-shirt, whether it was a boy or a girl, but whichever it was, it was excited to come play with Latte. The mother took a moment to realize her child had taken off, but when she did, she jumped up and started running across the playground.

"Doggie!" the little one squealed, moving faster than I thought a child that size could.

I was running, too. I wasn't worried about Latte hurting the child at all, both because of the fence separating them and because he was as sweet and docile as they come, but I was concerned that the child might get scared once he—or she—was up close and personal with Latte. I also didn't know how the mother would react with her child being so close to a strange dog.

"Latte! Sit!" I yelled. I felt that if he was sitting and responding to my commands, the mother would at least be able to see that he was a calm dog. Thankfully, Latte sat and even lifted one paw into his begging position. If I hadn't needed all my breath to propel my continued running, I would have breathed a sigh of relief.

The mother and I reached them at the same time.

"I am so sorry!" she panted, trying to catch her breath. She knelt down next to the child. "Don't run away like that. You can't try to play with doggies you don't know."

"It's okay," I assured her. "He wanted to play. He's really friendly. I think he saw your little one over there and thought they could be playmates."

"Doggie!" the child exclaimed, pointing at Latte. The child leaned into the mother and said something I couldn't hear.

"She wants to know if she can pet the dog," the mother said.

"Sure," I replied. "Let me just grab his leash." I jogged back over to where we'd been playing fetch and picked up the bright-blue leash. I went back to the gate, where Latte was still patiently waiting, paw in the air, for the tiny girl to pick up the ball and throw it for him. I hooked the leash onto Latte's collar and guided him back away from the inward-opening gate. "Sit, Latte," I instructed him, wanting to be sure that he behaved himself and didn't inadvertently scare the little girl. I wrapped the leash around my hand to keep him close then reached out and pulled the gate open. The little girl darted in, excited to get close to Latte.

"Emmy, stop. Wait!" the mother called out.

I couldn't believe what I'd just heard. "I'm sorry," I said. "Did you just call her Emmy?"

Chapter Seventeen

"Yes," the mother said, looking at me suspiciously. She grabbed Emmy's hand and pulled her back away from Latte and me.

"Doggie!" Emmy cried, pointing at Latte and straining from her mother's grasp.

"You're not Melissa, by any chance, are you?" I asked.

"Why?" She took a small step back, looking as though she was ready to run at a moment's notice.

"I'm friends with Samantha Eriksen. She works for me," I said. The woman seemed to relax, but only a little. "She told me about her friend Melissa and her daughter Emmy. If you're Melissa, I just wanted to introduce myself. And express my condolences. I'm Francesca Amaro. I run Antonia's Italian Café."

She became clearly more at ease, even letting Emmy, who had never stopped straining at her mother's hand, move toward Latte.

"Oh, you're Francesca? I knew your mom. She was wonderful. She loved Emmy to death." She stopped and blushed, realizing her unfortunate choice of words. "Oh my God, I'm so sorry," she muttered.

"It's okay," I said, marveling at how many casual death-related phrases there seemed to be and how that only became obvious when someone close passed away. "It's just a figure of speech."

"Still"—she held her free hand to her face, colored red with embarrassment—"I should know better."

"Really, it's okay. I know you didn't mean anything by it." I gave her a moment to compose herself. "So, you are Melissa?"

"Oh, yes. Sorry. Melissa Harris." She extended her hand for me to shake. "And you already know this is Emmy."

"Hi, Emmy," I said.

The little girl was ignoring us, making faces at Latte and laughing at his antics. My greeting did nothing to distract her.

"Emmy, say hello," Melissa said.

Emmy turned her big hazel eyes up to me. "Hello," she said in a clear little bell-like voice before turning her attention right back to Latte.

"Kids," Melissa said with a shrug.

I laughed. "Would she want to throw the ball for him?" I asked.

"Do you want to throw the ball for the doggie, Emmy?" Melissa asked, leaning down toward her.

"Yes!" she exclaimed.

I grabbed Latte's ball and closed the gate, latching it so it wouldn't swing back open, letting a dog or a child out. I unhooked Latte's leash from his collar and handed the ball to Emmy. She threw it as hard as she could, which wasn't really very hard, but Latte ran the five feet, picked it up, and ran it back to her, dropping it at her feet. She squealed with glee and threw it again. We watched them play for a few minutes, then Melissa stepped toward me.

"Did you know Joey?" she asked quietly. She had one arm folded across her chest as if to guard herself, and the other hand nervously played with her brown curls. Her blue eyes flitted to my face and then back away to where Emmy was playing with Latte.

"No, I didn't," I admitted. "His name was familiar, but he was a few years behind me in school, so I never really knew him. I was very sorry to hear, though."

"Thanks," she said quietly. "I was sorry about your mother."

"Thank you," I replied. We stood quietly for a minute. I wanted to find a way to ask her about Joe, but I couldn't quite figure out how to bring it up. "How are you doing?" I asked.

She took a moment to answer, and I wasn't quite sure she had heard me. "I'm making it," she said finally.

"And Emmy?"

Melissa sighed. "She doesn't really understand. He didn't live with us, so she's used to him not being around, but she still wants to call him on the phone and talk to him."

I decided to just go for it and ask about the murder. "Do the police have any suspects?" I asked, trying my best to sound casual.

"I don't really know," she said. "They don't really tell us what's going on with the investigation. And they talk to his parents more than me. 'Baby mama' apparently doesn't count as next of kin." She scoffed a little as she said it, but I could tell the situation bothered her.

She fell quiet, and I struggled to think of a way to ask about her own potential motive when she handed it to me.

"Of course, they sure didn't hesitate to rake me over the coals about where I was that night and whether I was angry that he wasn't paying child support. I was down at the police station for four hours on Tuesday. I was supposed to be planning Joey's funeral and comforting our daughter, but I was holed up in an interrogation room, telling some cops my life story."

"You didn't do it, did you?" I asked, making sure my voice was jovial enough that she didn't think I was accusing her.

"No," she exclaimed. "I loved Joey. Always have. Ever since back in high school. He just needed to get his life together, get a job—grow up, you know? He loved Em, but I don't think he'd really realized he was a father yet, like, a father who had responsibilities and all. He still wanted to act like he was a single guy."

"You said he wasn't paying child support?" We both had our eyes fixed on Emmy and Latte still playing with the ball, so I felt that asking tough questions was a little easier.

"Not really. On and off, like he'd pay a month here or there, but it wasn't regular like it was supposed to be. He hadn't paid in a while, but a couple of days before he died, he came and gave me two thousand dollars. I was almost afraid to ask where he got it, but I needed it. Emmy needs new clothes—she's wearing hand-me-downs from my cousin's little boy half the time. She loves glitter and sparkles and girlie stuff, but all she has is plain shorts and T-shirts. I try to at least put ribbons in her hair so she looks like a girl, but she always pulls them out." She looked over at me. "You don't think it was wrong of me to take the money, do you?"

"No, not at all! You need that money for your little girl. I don't fault you at all." And I didn't. My mother had been a single parent, too. She'd been lucky enough to live with my grandparents and rely partly on them, but she still needed every penny she could get, to keep me clothed and fed. I didn't judge any single mother's efforts to care for her child.

She sighed and gave me a halfhearted smile. "I think he was gambling," she said.

"Like casinos?"

"Sports. That was his thing. He understood sports. He could have been a professional athlete, I think, if he'd made some different choices."

"Do you think his..." I paused, not wanting to say the word *murder*, "his death was related to the gambling?"

"I don't know," she said, her voice barely over a whisper. The subject seemed hard for her to talk about, but at the same time, she seemed to want to vent. She probably hadn't had much of a chance over the past week to really talk about her feelings. "There was a guy at the gym..." she started before trailing off.

"He was having a problem with someone?"

"I don't know. Joey would never admit that he was having a problem or that he couldn't handle something. I worried about him kickboxing, though."

"You were afraid he'd get hurt?"

She shrugged. "That, yeah. And it was so violent. I know it's all supposed to be very controlled and all, but some of the guys he fought were kind of scary. I mean, Joey knew it wasn't personal, but I didn't know about some of those guys. There was this one guy Joey fought a couple of months ago, and I don't know what happened, because I never really understood how the kickboxing worked, like how much they were supposed to beat each other up and when they stopped the fight and all, but Joey just beat the guy to a pulp—broke his nose and everything. It scared me that Joey could hurt someone like that, but the guy, he's just a thug. And he was mad at Joey for beating him up like that."

"Do you think he could have done something to... to hurt Joe?" It occurred to me that I might have another suspect.

"I don't know." Melissa's voice was breaking. "Maybe. I don't want to think about it, but I'm afraid he might have."

"Do you know his name?" I asked.

She shook her head. "No," she said, practically in a whisper. "Joey didn't talk about it very much. I only heard about it in the first place because I overheard him telling someone about it on the phone. When I asked, he refused to tell me anything except that he was fine and there was nothing for me to worry about. I hate to think—" She cut herself off, apparently not wanting or finding herself able to say more.

I reached out and rubbed her arm to try to comfort her. She was practically a stranger, but I felt for her and what she was going through. She stared at Emmy and Latte, who were now chasing each other playfully in circles.

"It's good to see her having fun," she said softly. "She's been around a bunch of sad adults all week."

"Latte seems like he's having a lot of fun, too."

"His name's Latte?" Melissa asked with a smile.

"Yeah, I figured he was the right color."

"It's a great name," she said.

"Maybe we could get them together to play again sometime," I suggested. They really did seem to be having fun together. And even though I'd only known her for a little while, I felt I could be friends with Melissa.

"Yeah, that would be great!" A big smile spread across her face, and I could tell she genuinely liked the idea and wasn't just agreeing to it to appease me.

I glanced at the time on my phone and realized Latte and I had to get going so I could make it to work on time. Much to Emmy's dismay, I called Latte over and put his leash back on. I shoved the drool-coated tennis ball back in my pocket even though I knew I would regret that later. At least that was better than carrying it the whole way.

"Bye-bye, Emmy!" I said as Latte and I started toward the gate. A thought crossed my mind just before I walked out.

"Hey, Melissa," I called back to her. "Do you know Todd, the guy who owns the gym?"

Her previously bright face darkened. "Yes. Why?"

I realized I needed to be cautious. "I graduated high school with him. I know he owns the gym, so I thought I'd ask."

Melissa walked over to me and lowered her voice. "You know how I said I didn't really like Joey kickboxing?"

I nodded.

"Todd encouraged it. Todd filled Joey's head with the idea he could be really successful at it and make a living off of it. Joey would have quit a long time ago and focused on his night classes if Todd hadn't filled his head with all that nonsense. I told him right before he died—that night that he brought over the money—that I wanted him to stop, and I think he was going to. I think he was going to quit the night that he died. I don't know if he did or not, but I know Todd wouldn't have been happy about it. I don't know if Todd did something directly or indirectly to get Joey killed, but he wouldn't have been at that gym if Todd hadn't encouraged it. And if he hadn't been at the gym, he wouldn't have died. Maybe it's not fair, but I hold Todd responsible. I absolutely believe that if not for Todd, Joey would be here today."

I could tell by the fire in Melissa's face that she believed every word and believed so strongly I had to reevaluate my confidence in Todd's innocence.

Chapter Eighteen

Sammy was working with Rhonda at the café when I got in. Rhonda was a housewife in her late thirties who worked with us a few hours a week, mostly so she could say she had a job and so she could have a little pocket money to finance an occasional trip to the Neiman Marcus up in Boston. Generally, she worked while her kids were in school, so we hadn't seen much of her over the summer, but her husband was on his annual golf trip, and her kids were at their grandma's for the week, so she was picking up some extra hours. I also suspected she had her eye on something that cost a little more than two hours of work could pay for.

"Hello, ladies!" I said as I slipped my apron over my head and tied it. "How's everything been today?"

"Slow!" they both replied.

"That bad, huh?"

Sundays were always slow. We got a rush first thing in the morning and then around lunch, but other than that, Sundays were like a faucet that was turned down to a drip.

"Yes," Sammy said emphatically. "We were just debating which one of us should go home. I said Rhonda should go home and enjoy her quiet house—"

"But I told her that Louboutins don't pay for themselves," Rhonda interrupted.

So I was right—she did have her eye on something. Still, I wrinkled my nose at her mention of Louboutins.

"Prada makes lovely shoes," I said. "They have some really great ones in their fall collection." Thanks to my mother and grandmother, I was an exclusive purchaser of Italian leather. Growing up, I'd heard them extoll the virtues of the grain, the finish, and the stitching on shoes and bags made in Italy. It was so ingrained in me, I'd never been tempted by the ubiquitous shoes made by Christian Louboutin while I lived in New York.

"But Prada doesn't have those red soles!" Rhonda moaned. Her eyes were obviously already envisioning what it would be like for everyone to see that flash of red when she crossed her legs.

"You know the red wears off, right?" I asked.

"Yeah, but you can get them repaired. I think they even sell paint kits for you to do it yourself."

"If I paid that much for a pair of shoes, I don't think I'd be taking a paintbrush to them. Pay a professional for that," Sammy said.

"Or just buy Prada. Or Fendi. Or Ferragamo," I suggested.

"Nope, gotta be the Louboutins," Rhonda said.

Apparently, there was just no beating the allure of the scarlet soles of those shoes. Even I had to admit they looked nice, even if I wasn't interested in owning a pair myself.

"How about you both stay," I said. "At least for a little bit. I need taste testers. I've figured out what kind of tea drinks I think I want to add to the menu, but I want someone else's opinion first, to make sure I'm not the only one who likes them."

"All right, let's go!" Rhonda said enthusiastically. I knew she was more excited about the extra money she'd get for sticking around than she was about trying the new drinks.

"Sammy?" I asked.

"I'm in."

I went into the back and unloaded the box of tea and supplies I'd brought with me, arranging everything in the order necessary to prepare the drinks. I grabbed one of the French presses and the tin of Earl Grey tea and took them out front.

"So what are we having?" Sammy asked. She and Rhonda had gone around to the customer side of the counter, apparently looking forward to the experience of being waited on instead of doing the serving.

I measured out enough tea for three small drinks and dumped it into the center of the French press. I figured that if we were going to be sampling several drinks, we didn't need full-size helpings of each. I poured boiling water from the espresso machine into the press and closed the lid. After all my research and testing, I had come to the conclusion that black tea tasted best when the water was at a full boil when the steeping began. I glanced at the digital clock we used as a timer, to make sure I got the steeping time just right for my sample drinks.

"We are having a drink called a London Fog," I said finally as I started steaming the milk. I could practically steam milk in my sleep, so talking was easier while I did that.

"Sounds fancy!" Rhonda said, clearly enticed by the mention of the cosmopolitan city.

"What's in it?" Sammy asked, more practically.

"It's basically a latte, but with tea instead of coffee," I said, looking up from my steaming with a grin.

She laughed. "So you went with something comfortable."

"Of course!" I replied.

"So is it just tea and milk? Do we do tea latte art?"

"It is tea, steamed milk, vanilla, and sugar," I said, keeping my eye on the clock, not wanting to let the tea steep too long and get bitter. "I haven't really had success with the art. I don't think the tea's the right consistency. It doesn't have the crema like espresso does. I have a couple of ideas, though." I smiled at Sammy, guessing what her reaction would be.

"Of course you do," she said predictably. "I don't know what you'd do if you couldn't do something artistic with your drinks."

"That's because Francesca is very sophisticated," Rhonda interjected. She liked to call me by my full name because she thought it sounded more refined. "And the designs she puts into lattes makes the drinks look so sophisticated."

"Thank you, Rhonda," I said pointedly. "At least somebody appreciates me."

"Oh, stop!" Sammy laughed. "You know I think you do an amazing job."

"I just wanted to hear you say it," I replied.

Sammy rolled her eyes. "Isn't it time for you to do something else with that tea?" she asked.

It was. I slowly lowered the plunger in the French press, then turned the lid to open it. I filled each of the three cups I had laid out about a quarter of the way full and then added the milk. Sammy and Rhonda leaned across the counter, watching what I was doing. Sammy, in particular, was studying the process so she'd be able to recreate it later. When the cups were halfway full, I drizzled in some vanilla extract and then topped them off with a sprinkling of sugar before stirring it all together.

"Just enough so you can get the taste of the drink." I slid the cups over in front of them. "They'll be full when we serve them for real, of course."

I watched as Sammy lifted the cup to her nose and inhaled.

Apparently deciding she approved, she started to take a sip, but abruptly stopped before the cup touched her lips. She raised an eyebrow at me. "Aren't you going to try it?"

"What? You think I'm pranking you?" I laughed.

She kept her suspicious gaze on me until I relented, rolling my eyes. I picked up my cup and took a sip. It was as delicious as a drink that wasn't coffee could be. I nodded and put it down.

"Well?" Sammy asked.

"It's good," I said. "But I already know what I think. I want to know what you think."

Sammy and Rhonda finally tried their drinks. Sammy nodded approvingly, but Rhonda's eyes lit up.

"It's really good!" Rhonda exclaimed. She quickly downed the rest of the beverage.

Sammy sipped from her cup more slowly, savoring it. Finally, she spoke up. "I like it. I think it will be good on the menu."

"Good!" I replied, happy that my first offering had met with their approval. "On to the next!"

After all my experimenting, I had settled on the London Fog, a chai latte, and a green-tea latte. For customers who didn't want a latte, we would also serve plain hot tea. I felt those choices would provide enough variety to cater to different tastes while not adding too much bulk to the menu. I didn't want to add a ton of new products—just enough to diversify a little bit.

We went through each of the drinks and sampled them. Sammy and Rhonda had their favorites and their less-than-favorites, but overall, they agreed the selection would work well on our menu and wouldn't be any harder to fix than the drinks we already sold, which was important to them being successful. If they were great but took forever to make or were so complicated we could never get them right, no one would order them more than once, and all my effort would be for nothing.

We had only a couple of customers during the whole time we were testing drinks, so I was finally able to convince Rhonda to go home when we were done. I reminded her of how luxurious a long, hot bubble bath in a quiet house would be, and she was more than happy to go. I used the excuse that the menu board was in Sammy's handwriting to convince her to climb up and update it with the new tea drinks. I did want the board to be consistent, and I also wanted to avoid having my atrocious handwriting up there.

"Latte and I ran into Melissa and Emmy today," I told her as she wrote.

"You did?" Her tone told me she was more focused on her writing than on what I was saying. "I didn't think you knew them."

"I didn't before today. Latte and Emmy started trying to play, and when I heard her name, I realized who she was."

"Did you mention you knew me?"

"Yeah, Melissa seemed a little creeped out until I told her. I figured I should mention it to you in case you ran into her and she said something."

"Yep." She was completely absorbed by drawing a picture of a steaming cup of tea. She drew one final wisp of steam then stepped back to look at her work. "What do you think?" she asked me.

"It's pretty perfect," I replied. I was constantly in awe of Sammy's artistic skill.

"Thanks!" she chirped happily. Apparently satisfied that it was indeed pretty perfect, she climbed up the stepladder to hang the board back up.

I stood back from the counter, watching to make sure it was straight.

"Good?" she asked.

"Good."

She climbed back down.

"Do you need me to hang around, or are you good on your own?" she asked.

"Why? Do you have big plans tonight?" I teased.

She shrugged, but the blush on her cheeks told me she did.

"Ooh-ooh-ooh," I sing-songed like a middle schooler. "Hot date with Jared?"

Jared was her boyfriend, who in my opinion, had more flaws than charms, but they'd been together practically forever even though he refused to propose. His mother needed him to take care of her, he insisted.

"It's our anniversary. He said he has a surprise for me," she admitted, her blush deepening.

"A sparkly surprise?"

"I don't know. I mean..." She paused and took a breath. She'd gotten her hopes up before, I knew, and she was obviously trying to contain them to prevent disappointment. Finally, she shrugged. "A girl can hope."

"Go, then!" I urged, shooing her off.

She took off her apron, getting ready to leave, then paused. "Have you called Mike yet? About some kind of security?" She was asking for my sake since I'd be the one closing up.

I shook my head. "No, not yet." I cast a glance around the empty café. "But if it stays this busy, I may do it today."

"You should," Sammy said earnestly. "But, either way, be careful going home."

"I will," I assured her. "Now go. Get out. Go get all dolled up for your date. And have fun!" I was practically pushing her out the door, knowing she'd linger forever if I didn't.

"Okay." She laughed. "I'll see you tomorrow!"

"Bye!" I replied, waving her away. I watched her trip off down the sidewalk and then went back inside to find something in the vacant coffee shop to occupy myself with. It was only after she'd disappeared from view that I remembered wanting to ask her if she knew the name of the guy whose nose Joe had broken. I made a mental note to ask her the next day—about that and about her anniversary date.

Chapter Nineteen

The rest of that day was predictably slow, but the next day was surprisingly busy. We were never that busy on Mondays, but that day, we were slammed. Sammy actually called me to come in early because it was so hectic. I could pretend that word had gotten out about the new items on the menu and people were flocking in to get them, but it was far more likely that the weather was driving them in, actually. The day was gray and on the cool side, not exactly ideal beach weather.

The new drinks were as popular as anything else on the menu. Sammy had added them to the chalkboards out front and on the counter so people would notice we had them. Most of the people who came in were tourists and didn't know that the tea lattes were new, but a few locals came in and tried them over their regular drinks. They all seemed pretty pleased with their orders, and I was glad I had chosen the ones I had. I made a mental note to e-mail Rose Howard, the Englishwoman who had given me the idea to enhance our tea offerings, to let her know we would be much better prepared the next time she came in.

Things were blessedly slowing down, though still busy, when Jack walked in, dressed as much like a stereotypical tourist as ever.

"Hi, Jack!" I called to him as I glanced up from my place behind the counter. "I got that tea added to the menu."

"I saw that," he replied in his thick Southern accent. "Which one do you recommend?"

"My favorite's the Earl Grey—the London Fog—but Rhonda has her own thoughts." I nodded at Rhonda standing at the cash register.

"Oh my God, the chai! It's amazing!" she gushed.

Jack laughed as he approached the register. "How about I try one of each?"

"You may as well get all three, then," Rhonda suggested. "Try the full range."

Jack laughed again, at her not-so-subtle attempt to upsell him. "Sure, why not?"

"Let me know what you think," I urged him.

"Don't worry, I will." He smiled.

Sammy and I set about preparing the drinks as Rhonda took the next order.

I was a little disappointed that, after he finished his drinks, he left without telling me what he thought of them. I hoped he'd be back sometime so I could ask his opinion. He seemed like something of a connoisseur of coffee and cafés, so I figured that I could please anyone if I could please him.

"Wasn't he here last week?" Sammy asked quietly as he walked out the door. "The day they found Joe's body?"

"Yeah." I nodded as I worked on preparing a customer's drink.

"That's a long stay for a tourist."

I shrugged as I handed her a cup to take out to the table we'd been preparing drinks for. "He said he's spending the summer travelling along the New England coast. I guess he just liked us enough to stay for a while."

Sammy seemed to accept my answer and took the drinks out to the waiting customers. We worked on steadily for a couple more hours until Rhonda had to leave so she could get a shower and get ready to go out to dinner with a friend. Fortunately, traffic in and out of the café had slowed down even more, and Sammy and I were able to handle it with no problem. In fact, I was getting ready to send her home when the bell over the door jingled and a slightly overweight middle-aged man in a warm-up jacket came in. I felt he looked familiar—an older version of someone I used to know—but I couldn't be sure whether he was actually someone I used to know or his father.

Sammy immediately greeted him warmly. "Hi, Coach Snyder!"

As soon as she said it, I remembered him. Steve Snyder had been the baseball coach and history teacher at Cape Bay High School for as long as I could remember. In a small town like ours, the varsity sports coaches were local celebrities. Everyone knew them and called them "Coach" whether they'd gone to the high school or not.

"Hi, Coach," I said.

"Hi, Sammy. Hi, Franny," Coach replied as he approached the counter. His tone was subdued, and I wondered if everything was okay. I was about to ask when Sammy spoke up.

"How's retirement treating you, Coach?"

"You know, it's not as easy as I thought it would be," he replied. "I'm used to spending summers writing football plays and checking in on my players, not piddling around, looking for things to do."

Sammy nodded sympathetically. "I can imagine that's difficult." She paused, tipped her head down, and leaned toward him. "And Joe. That must be hard for you, too."

Coach tensed as though someone had punched him. He closed his eyes and swallowed hard. When he finally opened his eyes, he nodded. "Yes," he said hoarsely. "I don't... Joe was a good kid. Back when I coached him, I thought he had a good chance to make it as a ballplayer. I still can't believe—" He broke off and shook his head. "He was a good kid."

Sammy and I waited quietly while he composed himself. A week wasn't much time to process a sudden death. Sammy still had her moments when she had to pause and take a deep breath, and Melissa had certainly still been deeply emotional. My heart went out to him.

"Well," he said finally. "I didn't come here to make two young ladies feel sorry for an old man. I came here to get something to eat. Let me get a..." He took a moment to scan the menu, rubbing his hand absently as he scanned its offerings. "I'll take a tea and a tiramisu."

"What kind of tea would you like?" Sammy asked.

Coach stared at her blankly.

"We have Earl Grey, chai, and—"

"I just want a regular iced tea," Coach interrupted.

Sammy looked at me.

"I'll take care of it," I said quickly. I hadn't planned for anyone ordering iced tea, although I should have. For the moment, I decided to just make a strong Earl Grey tea and pour it over ice. If it tasted good, that's what I would plan on doing every day. At least we could make iced tea ahead of time and serve it throughout the day.

My plan seemed to work out well enough. Coach did declare the beverage "different," but that was to be expected since Earl Grey isn't typically used for iced tea. Still, he drank it all down without complaint, and I considered it a success. In the hope that the tea would be good, I'd used my large, fifty-ounce French press to make the tea, so I poured it out into a pitcher and put it into the refrigerated case to chill.

"Sammy?" I gave her a charming smile.

"Yes?" she replied, knowing I was about to ask her to do something.

"Could you add *iced* tea to the menu for me?"

She laughed brightly at my second request for an update in as many days. Before that, I didn't think she'd had to make any changes to it in months, perhaps longer. "Of course, Franny. I'd be happy to," she said, her tone making it clear that she had seen my question coming.

She went and got her chalk and added the words "iced tea" to the menu.

"If you keep adding stuff, we're going to have to get another board," she commented as she drew. She was filling in an empty space at the bottom of the board with a remarkably lifelike picture of a glass of iced tea.

"Stop acting like you wouldn't love having more space to draw," I retorted.

"You got me." She added a small spot of white chalk to one of the ice cubes and declared her work finished.

A customer who had been lingering in an armchair got up and left, leaving Sammy and me alone in the café for the first time all afternoon.

"So, how was your anniversary surprise?" I asked as soon as the door closed behind the woman.

Sammy's previously cheery countenance turned to a scowl. "Go-karts. My big surprise was go-karts."

"For your anniversary?"

"Yup. And surprise, surprise, heels aren't the best footwear for driving them."

I nodded, seeing how that would be a problem.

"Jared had fun anyway." She shrugged.

"So no sparkly jewelry?"

"No sparkly jewelry."

I decided to abandon being a neutral observer. "Why are you still with him?" I asked.

Sammy turned her big blue eyes to mine. "Because I love him."

I returned her gaze for a moment, gauging her sincerity. "Well, I can't argue with that," I said finally.

We spent the next several minutes cleaning up everything we'd failed to attend to during the rush. It wasn't that things were dirty or messy—the health inspector still would have passed us easily—but they weren't quite up to our standards.

I was putting some clean towels away in a cabinet in the back room when I turned suddenly and smacked my nose on the cabinet's open door. It hurt, but it also reminded me of something I wanted to ask Sammy.

Holding a paper towel to the nick on my nose, I went out front to where Sammy was scrubbing down the counter.

"Are you okay?" she asked.

"Yeah, just hit my nose on the cabinet door."

Sammy shook her head.

"But, speaking of noses, do you know anything about Joe Davis breaking some guy's nose in a kickboxing match a couple of months back?"

"Not a thing," she said, giving the counter one last swipe with her rag. "Do you need anything else before I get out of here?" She had opened the café that morning, as she did most mornings, and had by then put in more than her time for the day.

I looked over at the clock. "Actually, could you hang out for another half hour or so? I need to run home and let Latte out real quick since I came in so early."

"Not a problem," Sammy said. "And if it stays this busy, the place will be spick-and-span by the time you get back."

"An added benefit." I smiled. I took off my apron and grabbed my purse from the back. "I shouldn't be long." I hurried out and down the street. The break would give me time to think about where else I might be able to find out who Joe had beaten up.

Chapter Twenty

I only figured it out late the next day, although not through my own ingenuity.

I was alone in the café when Todd came in.

"Hey, Franny," he called as he walked through the door.

"Hi, Todd," I called back. "What can I do for you today?"

"Is your iced tea sweetened?"

"Does this look like Mississippi?" I joked. "I can add sweetener for you if you'd like, but otherwise it's unsweetened."

"A glass of tea then, please." Todd seemed to be in a much better mood than he had been the past few times I'd seen him.

"Not a problem," I replied. I grabbed a glass, filled it with ice, and poured the tea I'd made earlier in the day over it. As it turned out, iced tea was more popular than I'd expected, and I was already on the third pitcher. I wondered why we'd never put it on the menu before. Tradition, I supposed. "Can I get you anything else?"

"How about dinner?" he asked, leaning across the counter toward me.

I stared at him, completely confused. "Well, we have mozzarella-tomato-basil sandwiches and a tomato salad, but other than those, unless you want a piece of tiramisu or a—"

"How about you come out to dinner with me?" Todd corrected, interrupting me.

"Oh," I said as it was the only thing I could think to say. I thought for a few seconds, debating whether to accept. Matt wouldn't be getting back until the next day, so I didn't have any other plans for dinner. I didn't want Todd to get the impression that I had a romantic interest in him, but he'd asked if I would go out, not if he could take me out, so that might not have even crossed his mind. Finally, I realized that he was sure to know who had been in that kickboxing match gone wrong. "Sure. I don't close up for a couple of hours yet—is it okay if we have a late dinner?"

"Of course!" He grinned. "How about I come back by for you then?"

"Sounds good," I replied.

He drank his tea down quickly, a skill I guessed he had picked up over years of chugging beer.

"That's good," he said, setting the glass down on the counter. He headed for the door, his long legs carrying him quickly across the room. "I'll see you soon!" he called just as he went out the door.

I waved idly at his back. The way he had appeared in the café, invited me to dinner, and disappeared all within five minutes had thrown me off balance. Had he come in just to ask me to dinner? Or had he come in to get something to drink and suggested dinner on the spur of the moment? Whichever it was, it seemed strange. I distracted myself from thinking about it by remembering that I could use the opportunity to ask him not just about the man whose nose Joe broke, but also about some of the other things Melissa had mentioned to me as we talked in the park.

I worked my way around the café, straightening things up so I could leave quickly when Todd came back. I felt as though I was forever wiping down tables, adjusting chairs, and washing dishes, but I supposed that was to be expected. I checked the display cases to make sure they were fully stocked for the next morning, grateful Monica had insisted in bringing a fresh delivery of tiramisu each day—it had continued to sell stunningly well. A couple of customers came in and lingered over cups of coffee before heading back out into the night.

I was wondering where Todd was and was getting ready to lock up when he burst through the door.

"Hey, Franny. You ready to go?"

"Yup. Just about," I replied. I looked around to make sure everything was in order and ready for Sammy to hit the ground running in the morning. Satisfied that everything was in good shape, I took off my apron and grabbed my purse and keys. "Do you mind if we run by my house real quick so I can feed the dog and let him out?"

"I didn't know you had a dog."

"Yup. Just got him a few months ago."

"Sweet. I love dogs."

We stepped outside onto the sidewalk, and I locked up.

"My car's right here." He gestured to a dark-blue convertible muscle car pulled up to the curb. It was a cool 1960's-era car, probably something recognizable to someone who knew more about cars than I did.

I was surprised to see that he'd driven. "Where are we going to eat?" I asked, thinking it must be someplace out of town.

"I thought we'd go to the Mexican place down on the beach. Do you like that place? They have great food there."

"I love that place," I said, wondering why he'd driven his car if that was as far as we were going, but I guessed maybe he didn't think I would want to walk, or maybe he'd driven somewhere else before coming back by. I didn't remember having seen his car when he'd been at the café earlier in the day, but I hadn't really been looking, either. As we got in the car, I thought of yet another possibility—perhaps Todd, too, was conscious of there still being no arrest in Joe's murder. Perhaps Todd was even afraid he might be in danger as well.

Todd revved the engine higher than he needed to and pulled the car away from the curb, making a U-turn in the middle of the street to direct it toward my house. I knew some girls liked it when guys showed off their cars like that, but just as I didn't know one old car from another, I didn't know why revving engines and squealing tires were appealing.

The trip to my house was quick in the car. I was surprised I didn't have to give Todd a single direction on the way there.

"How did you know where I live?" I asked as we pulled into my driveway.

"Same place as in high school," Todd said.

"You knew where I lived back when we were in high school?"

"Course I did," he replied, climbing out of the car. He was almost to the front door by the time I made it out of my seat. I scurried to catch up.

Latte burst through the door as soon as I opened it, first prancing around our feet and then sniffing Todd intently. I went ahead inside and scooped Latte's food into his bowl. The sound of the bits of kibble falling into the ceramic bowl drew him away from Todd, and he rushed into the kitchen to gobble down his dinner. Todd followed him in.

"Haven't gotten around to redecorating yet, huh?"

"Nope, not yet," I replied. "I'm hoping to be able to spend a little more time on it after the season ends."

"You should. It looks like an old person lives here instead of a beautiful, eligible bachelorette."

I wasn't sure whether I should be offended or flattered, so I laughed his remark off without comment.

"Latte, let's go outside. M–" I cut myself off before referring to myself as "Mommy" in front of Todd. "I'm going out for a little bit." Latte ran back outside and then back in. "We'll go for a walk when I get back, okay?" I said as I closed the door behind me.

"You should be careful walking alone late at night," Todd warned. "You don't know what kind of creeps could be out roaming the streets. A defenseless woman like you would be an easy target."

"I'm not defenseless," I retorted, bristling at his implication. "I lived in New York for years, remember? I know how to take care of myself."

"Yeah, but Joe was a semipro kickboxer, and you know what happened to him."

The way Todd said it made me uneasy, and I was tired of being uneasy, of being always on edge as I wondered who had killed Joe and if it was random and if the guy was still out there. I needed to buckle down and get serious about finding out who was responsible for Joe's death. The time for just poking around was over.

We got into his car, which he drove slowly down the residential street.

"Have you heard anything else from the police?" I asked.

"Old Mikey keeps coming around, making sure I haven't skipped town or anything, but I think he's out of evidence. He's not asking any new questions. Just the same old ones: 'You haven't thought of anyone who can corroborate your story, have you?' 'Has anything come to mind about someone who might have had a grudge against Joe?'

I'm getting tired of it. I practically ignore him when he shows up now."

"That doesn't seem like it's the best way to get him on your side."

"Whatever." He scoffed. "I don't even care anymore. Mike can think whatever he wants."

"Even if he thinks you murdered Joe?"

"Nothing I can do to stop him."

I stared at him in stunned silence. If I had been accused of murder, I would do everything in my power to fight it. I'd present every shred of evidence I could find to prove my innocence. There's no way I'd just shrug my shoulders and say the police could think whatever they wanted. Unless, maybe—and I could hardly conceive of it—unless I actually did it.

I stared out the windshield at the orangey-yellow streetlights flickering by as we drove down Main Street. It was the first time I'd really entertained the thought that Todd might be guilty. When I thought about it, it made sense. He had the motive—Joe's months-overdue gym dues. He had the means and the opportunity—he knew better than anybody that the corner of the parking lot where Joe was killed was the poorest lit, that teenagers left their old broken beer bottles there, and that the security-camera system was down. He had a stereotypically bad alibi—home alone, watching TV. Despite the heat, I felt a chill go down my spine.

I might've been sitting in a car with a murderer.

Chapter Twenty-One

We sat across from each other at a table on the patio overhanging the water. It was late enough that we were the only ones there. Eating there with Matt had been romantic, but I felt uneasy, even afraid, sitting there with Todd. Even though I knew I was being dramatic, I was grateful for the screen enclosing the porch—if Todd tried to throw me into the ocean, I would leave a me-sized hole in the screen for the police to find. I looked around to find any security cameras, hopefully ones that worked.

"What are you looking for?" Todd asked.

"Just looking around," I said quickly.

"Seemed like you were looking for something."

I shrugged. "Nope, just looking around."

Todd seemed to believe me, because he went back to looking at his menu.

I wasn't sure that he had murdered Joe, but I knew this was my chance to find out. We were alone but in a fairly public place. He couldn't do anything to hurt me there, and if he did, plenty of people would hear me scream. It was now or never, but I couldn't just ask him outright. I had to work my way up to it.

"So, I ran into Joe's ex-girlfriend Melissa the other day."

He didn't take his nose out of the menu. "You did, huh?"

"Yeah, at the park. I was there with Latte, and he wanted to play with her little girl—"

"Wait, your latte wanted to play with Emmy?" He looked at me as if he thought I had lost my mind.

"Yeah, and—"

"How does a latte play with a child?"

"No, not *a* latte. Latte. My dog."

"Your dog's name is Latte?" he asked.

"Yeah."

"Huh," he grunted and looked back down at his menu.

I was sure I had said Latte's name in front of Todd earlier at the house, but maybe he had just missed it. "Anyway, I ran into Melissa, and we got to talking, and she said that—"

"I didn't know you knew Melissa," Todd said, interrupting me yet again.

"I didn't," I said, trying to hide my annoyance. "I just met her the other day."

"Oh."

I glared at the top of Todd's head as he continued studying the menu.

"*Anyway*," I repeated, hoping I could finish what I was trying to say that time. "She and I got to talking, and she mentioned that Joe had broken some guy's nose in a kickboxing match a couple of months ago."

"Yeah," Todd chuckled. "Dave Dean. Dude's big and slow. I don't know why he wanted to fight Joe. He knew he'd lose."

"Melissa said that Dave was upset about losing. Like he might do something to try to get back at Joe?"

"You're asking if I think Dave could have killed Joe? I just told you that he's big and slow, and Joe could take him in a fight *easy.*"

"Well, yeah, but Joe was stabbed."

"Not by Dave, trust me. Only way Joe let himself get stabbed like that is he didn't think the guy was a threat."

Like if it was his friend the gym owner. I had to take a different tack, though. "What if the guy was a better fighter than Joe?"

"He got stabbed, not beaten to death. Guy wouldn't have to stab him if he was winning."

He had a point there. But nothing he'd said had ruled himself out. As far as I knew, Todd wasn't a kickboxer, so he wouldn't have been a better fighter than Joe, and he and Joe were friends, so Joe wouldn't have seen the attack coming. Todd had even ruled out my next best suspect, Dave Dean, on the basis of Joe not letting his guard down around him.

I wasn't sure where to go next with my questioning. I didn't think I should outright accuse him or ask more probing questions about Todd's potential motive just yet. I was afraid he would shut me out if I moved too fast. I had to play it cool, even if I found it nerve-wracking to think that I might be sitting across from a murderer.

Fortunately, the waitress came and saved me from having to make a decision just yet. We ordered our food, and Todd got a beer. I ordered my standard margarita. When the waitress left, I decided to ask my next question, also inspired by something Melissa had mentioned.

"Do you know if Joe gambled at all?" I asked.

Todd took a deep breath and dropped his head back to look at the ceiling. I almost thought he hadn't heard me and what I thought was his reaction was just a perfectly timed but completely unrelated action. Finally, though, he answered.

"Yeah, he did." He looked into my eyes. "Did Melissa tell you that, too?"

I nodded. I wasn't sure if he thought it was good or bad that Melissa had told me.

"I figured. You know, some guys—a lot of guys—can do it no problem. They keep to the slots or to blackjack, they play a few games, maybe lose a little money, and they walk away. Some guys who bet sports like Joe just hold off until they can get out to Vegas. Joe though, man... Joey couldn't stop himself. It wasn't something I talked to him about much, but I know he had a bookie, and you know, from some of what I heard, I think he was actually starting to make book himself."

"Make book?" I repeated. "What does that mean?"

"It means instead of him placing bets with someone else, guys were placing bets with him."

"That's illegal, isn't it?"

Todd laughed. "So is placing the bets with someone else."

"Is it dangerous?"

"If you don't have the money to pay out, it can be. The kind of money some of these guys wager on one game could pay for a year of their kids' private-school tuition. You take that bet and can't pay out, somebody's not going to be happy."

"Do you know who was making bets with Joe?" I asked. If what Todd was saying was true, and Joe had gotten in over his head, that might have been what got him killed. But that didn't do me any good unless I knew who was placing bets with him.

"No," Todd said emphatically. "I stayed out of it. I made sure he knew I didn't want that stuff going on in my gym, and then I walked away. Plausible deniability. If he ever got caught, I wasn't going down with him."

"Did you tell the cops?"

"I did. I hope they're looking into it. I guess they haven't found anything."

Another dead-end lead—at least for the time. I thought I could still find a way to figure out who else was involved in the betting, even if the cops hadn't. But that only mattered if Todd wasn't the one who killed Joe. And that was something I still had to figure out.

The waitress brought out our drinks. As I sipped my margarita, I thought about how I could bring the conversation back around to Todd himself and his involvement, or lack thereof, in Joe's murder. My fingers danced on the stem of my glass as I thought.

"You all right there?" Todd asked. "You look a little anxious."

I looked up from my glass at him, sitting across from me. His deep-blue eyes met mine unflinchingly. I was struck by the sadness there that I hadn't noticed before.

I wondered whether Joe's death or maybe the investigation was getting to him—or perhaps I was seeing his regret over having killed Joe.

"I'm okay. Are you?" I asked, hoping my tone conveyed a genuine question, not idle small talk.

It must have worked. His eyes held mine for a moment longer and then turned down to his beer bottle. "It's been a rough week," he said hoarsely.

"You've had a lot to deal with," I agreed.

"You don't even know. The girl I was seeing broke it off with me because she said it was too stressful knowing the cops are investigating me."

"That's kind of..." I paused, searching for the right word. "Crummy of her. I didn't even realize you were dating anyone. It's too bad you weren't with her the night of the murder."

He looked up at me, his face utterly stricken.

"Oh my God, you were! Why didn't you tell me? Have you told the police?"

"No." He looked back down at the table.

"Why on earth not?"

"I didn't... I wanted to protect her."

"But Todd, you're being investigated for murder! What could you possibly be protecting her from that's worth a murder charge?"

"I never thought it would go this far. I thought they would've figured out who really did it by now and it wouldn't matter."

"But it has gone this far," I exclaimed. "You have to tell them."

"I can't. I can't do that to her! I promised!"

"So what? She already broke up with you. What's going to happen if you tell the police you were with her?"

"I don't know... I mean, I don't want..." he stammered. "Her parents—"

"Wait, what?" I interrupted. "Her *parents*? She's not a teenager, is she? Please tell me she's out of high school." I thought of Becky and Amanda, the high schoolers who worked for me at the café, and prayed that the girl wasn't either of them—and also, if it was, that they hadn't met Todd in the café. I'd feel so guilty.

"She's out of high school," he said. "She's nineteen."

"Well, at least there's that." I shook my head and took another sip of my margarita. Suddenly, something clicked. I caught my breath. "It's Karli, isn't it? You're dating Karli." It made so much sense—Todd's enthusiasm for Karli's work, her distress at the repeated police business.

Todd hung his head. "I *was*," he muttered.

I didn't know what to say. She was so... young. And, in comparison, Todd and I were not. Todd was practically old enough to be her father, if he'd been a teen dad. Finally, I managed to focus my brain on the critical issue, Todd's alibi. I took a deep breath.

"So the issue was that you were afraid of her parents finding out that she was with you that night?"

Todd nodded. "She told them she was at a girlfriend's."

"Did they not like you two seeing each other, or did you just not want them to find out?" I asked, momentarily distracted again by the sordid details of Todd dating a teenager.

"They had an idea that we were going out, and her dad especially made it clear that he didn't like it. He didn't like that I'm closer to his age than to hers."

I bit my tongue to keep from muttering what I was thinking, which was *No kidding*. When I thought of something more polite to say, I spoke.

"Her parents don't have to know just because you tell the police. She's over eighteen. She can talk to the police without telling her parents a thing about it."

"I don't know... I mean—" Todd started.

"Todd! This is your *life*. You have to tell them. Now, whether they believe you or not since you've been lying to them all this time, I don't know. I mean, it's not like you have a hotel receipt or anything to prove you were out of town."

Todd dropped his head to stare at the table again.

"You're not serious," I said. "You have a receipt? Why didn't you just show it to them? You could have gotten yourself off the suspect list a long time ago."

"It has charges for room service," he replied. "The cops would've known I was there with somebody and wanted to talk to her."

"This is ridiculous." I buried my face in my hands and wondered if, despite Todd's apparent business prowess, the dumb-jock stereotype was true and he just really didn't understand what was at stake here and how weak his excuses were. I didn't want to debate it anymore. If Todd was going to act like a child, I was going to treat him like one. "Todd, this is outright ridiculous. You have to go to the police. Tomorrow morning, you're going to call Mike and tell him that you have new information, and you're going to take that hotel receipt and show it to him. Do you understand?"

He nodded reluctantly.

"You'll be lucky if Mike doesn't throw you in jail just for being a numbskull."

He nodded again. The waitress brought out our food, providing me with a convenient distraction from continually mulling over Todd's stupidity.

"You know," Todd said after a couple of bites, "I could really use a woman like you in my life—someone who doesn't take any nonsense, someone with a good head on her shoulders, someone my age."

Fifteen years ago, I would have given my right arm to hear him say that. But now? After the conversation we'd just had?

"Thank you, Todd. I take that as a compliment. But it's not going to happen."

"What? Why not?" His face had a sad-puppy-dog look on it that even a few hours before might have set me weak in the knees but presently held no sway over me. I got the sense that he didn't have much experience getting turned down.

I shook my head. "I just don't think we're right for each other."

"It's Matt, isn't it?" he asked. "I've heard you and him have a little bit of a thing going. Maybe if that goes south..."

I put aside my surprise that there were rumors about Matt and me going around Cape Bay—it was a small town, so what did I expect?—and focused on making sure he knew my rejection wasn't about Matt—not really, anyway.

"You're just not the right guy for me, Todd. A good friend, yes, but I'm not interested in you romantically."

Todd looked glumly at his plate. "Well, if you ever change your mind..."

"Thank you, but I don't think I will."

We focused on eating for the next few minutes and slowly picked up a conversation that was mercifully unrelated to Joe Davis or my romantic inclinations. When we were finished, Todd paid because he said he "owed it to me for smacking some sense into him." I wasn't going to argue with that.

When we got back to my place, he parked his car in the driveway and walked me up to the door.

"Thank you, Franny, for helping me realize I needed to tell the cops the truth." He reached down and enveloped me in a warm hug, holding me close for longer than strictly necessary before slowly letting me go. "I guess I'll see you around."

"Yeah, since you won't be getting thrown in jail for murder now."

"Hopefully, Mike isn't too hard on me for holding out on him for so long."

"I'm sure he'll be fair with you."

"All right, well, I'd better get going. Bye, Franny." Todd headed down my front walk and hopped into his car. It roared to life, and Todd backed it out of the driveway.

As it disappeared down the street, I heard footsteps coming toward me from across the neighbor's lawn. Every muscle in my body tensed as I tried to figure out if I could get the door unlocked and get inside before whoever it was could get to me.

Chapter Twenty-Two

The figure came into the light, and I saw with relief that it was Matt, home early from his business trip. I tensed up again as soon as I realized what he must have just seen.

"Franny? Were you just on a date with Todd?"

"Matt," I exclaimed. "I thought you weren't getting back until tomorrow."

"So you figured it would be a good time to go out on a date with Todd?" Matt asked.

"No, that's not what it was—"

"Really? It's not? Because I could see you pretty clearly in the porch light there, and that hug looked pretty cozy."

"Well, yeah, but—"

"But what?"

"But it wasn't a date!"

"Then what was it?"

"Todd just asked me to go to dinner with him."

"So it was a date."

In the spirit of the evening, I realized that it was utterly ridiculous for us to be standing in my front yard after ten o'clock at night, debating whether or not my dinner with Todd qualified as a date. I heaved a sigh. "Just come inside, okay?"

I unlocked the door and pushed it open for Matt to go in. Latte, of course, came rushing out, eager both to greet me and Matt and to empty his bladder. When he'd completed the latter, I called him back inside and shut the door behind the three of us.

Matt was standing in my living room, arms folded across his chest, looking rather unhappy.

"It wasn't a date," I said.

He just looked at me, silently daring me to convince him.

I walked into the living room and flicked the light on so we weren't standing in darkness. I sat down on the couch and motioned for Matt to join me. He instead sat down in an armchair off to the side.

"Todd came into the café today and asked me if I wanted to go get dinner tonight," I said.

Matt's glower didn't change.

"I said yes because I didn't see why not. I thought you were out of town"—Matt started to say something, but I raised my hand to stop him so I could finish—"which meant I didn't have any plans, and I had some new leads I wanted to ask him about. It seemed like a good opportunity. And it was. I got a lot of good information."

"All of which makes Todd look completely innocent, I'm sure."

"Actually, on our way over to dinner, he had me pretty convinced that he was guilty."

"I take it that didn't last," he said snidely.

"Well, no, not after he admitted he had an alibi."

"'Admitted?' Having an alibi isn't something people usually 'admit' to. They usually offer it up the first time the police so much as look at them."

"Yeah, well, Todd's kind of dumb, at least about this."

That got a laugh out of Matt.

"Yeah," I said. "He even has a receipt to prove where he was."

Matt's eyes widened in amazement. "And why didn't he tell the police this?"

"Because," I said then paused for dramatic effect, "his teenage girlfriend didn't want her parents to find out she was with him and not at her friend's house."

Matt stared at me open-mouthed for a few seconds, as incapable of processing what I'd just told him as I had been when Todd told me earlier in the evening. Then the look changed. "It's not–" he started then stopped. "You don't know her name, do you?"

I nodded, not sure why he was asking. "Karli."

He closed his eyes briefly and shook his head. "You've got to be kidding me."

"You know her?" I asked.

"The receptionist at Todd's Gym, right?"

"Yes, but how do you know her?"

Matt shrugged. "I've been going to the gym some."

"You have?" I asked, incredulous.

"Yeah, you know, I figured it would be good for me to get in shape some. That and I figured I might be able to pick up some gossip about what happened to Joe."

"And have you?"

"Actually, yeah. Apparently, he was pretty deep into betting on sports."

"That's what I heard, too!" I exclaimed. "Joe's ex-girlfriend Melissa and Todd both told me that he was involved in it. Melissa told me that a couple of days before he died, he came and gave her two thousand dollars. He didn't say where he got it, but she was guessing it was gambling money."

"He must have won pretty big to have gotten that kind of money out of it."

"Todd said he thought Joe was starting to take bets himself, from other people."

"I heard that too," Matt confirmed. "Somebody would have had to win *really* big to have made Joe that much money."

"Any idea who?" I asked.

"Not a clue."

We sat there for a few minutes, and I thought about whether there was anything else I knew that I needed to share with Matt. I assumed he was thinking along the same lines until he spoke up.

"I'm sorry I accused you of going on a date with Todd," he said.

"Yeah, what was with that?" I asked. "That was weird."

Matt shrugged and looked at the carpet. "I just don't like the idea of you going out with him."

"Even as friends?"

"No, friends is fine. I mean, as long as he knows that's all it is."

"Trust me, he knows."

Matt looked at me with an eyebrow raised, obviously questioning my assertion.

"He knows, Matty," I repeated firmly.

"But what about you, Franny?" He moved from the armchair over to the couch, beside me.

"Well, I'm the one who told him, so yeah, I think I know." My lips twitched as I held back a smile.

"Are you sure?"

"Yes, I'm sure."

A smile played at Matt's lips, but before he could say or do anything, Latte hopped up on the couch between us and leaned into Matt. He shoved his head under Matt's hand and snuffled until Matt started petting him.

"How are you, boy?" Matt asked Latte. "Were you good for your mommy while I was gone?"

I laughed at Matt referring to me as "Mommy." There were times that I thought Matt loved Latte every bit as much as I did, if not more.

"I thought you weren't coming back until tomorrow."

"I wasn't," Matt replied between tousles of Latte's ears. "But our last meeting of the day was canceled, and the one before it ended early, so I called the airline to see if they had any seats available on an earlier flight. And, what do you know, here I am! It'll be good to get to sleep in my own bed. Besides, I missed you."

I stared at him for a moment, scarcely believing what I'd just heard. We'd been tiptoeing around defining our relationship for several weeks, and I was pretty sure his saying he'd missed me while he was in Virginia was the closest he'd come to actually coming out and declaring his feelings for me.

"Matteo Cardosi, did you just admit that you missed me while you were gone?" I asked.

"Hmm?" Matt looked up at me innocently. "Oh, no, I was talking to Latte." He looked back down at Latte before his smile could totally betray his feigned innocence.

Matt played with Latte for a few minutes, the two of them eventually graduating to playing fetch with a stuffed rabbit toy while my thoughts drifted back to Joe.

"So where do you think we should go next in the investigation?" I eventually asked Matt.

He fought the toy bunny away from Latte and tossed it across the room. "Well, if I were talking to anyone but you, I would say we forget about it and let the police take care of it. But since I am talking to you, I'm not sure what we do. Is the gambling thing the only lead you have?"

I nodded. "And I don't really know where to go next with that. I don't have any names or anything."

"I could try to ask around at the gym a little more," Matt offered. "See if any of the guys know anything."

"Oh, they're 'the guys' now, huh?" I teased.

"Well, they're not girls," he shot back.

"I think you talking to them will be a good plan. I'm kind of at a loss otherwise. I might try talking to Sammy, but I've been trying to keep her out of it since Joe was her friend."

Matt nodded in agreement. We were both uncomfortable knowing a murderer was on the loose, but we were fully aware of how much worse the situation was when the victim of said murderer was a loved one. He looked over at the clock on the wall and cringed when he saw the time.

"I better get going." He stood. "Just because I wasn't supposed to be back until tomorrow afternoon doesn't mean they don't expect me at the office bright and early."

I was a little disappointed that he couldn't stay longer, but I understood and knew I probably needed to get to bed before long myself. I stood up and gave Matt a hug.

"Welcome back," I said softly. "I missed you."

"Don't tell Latte, but I missed you too," he replied.

I walked him to the door and said good night.

Chapter Twenty-Three

I didn't talk to Sammy at the café the next day, partly because I couldn't quite bring myself to ask her about her friend's gambling habit, which she may not have even known about, and partly because the café was steadily busy and we were never alone. The topic wasn't something tourists would find particularly appetizing. Eventually, work started to slow down, Sammy's shift ended, and my chance to ask her any questions was gone for the day.

I was alone when Coach Snyder came in again. I wanted to thank him for inadvertently getting me to put iced tea on the menu, but he was on his phone, seeming rather anxious as he talked to whoever was on the other end. I served him his tea and sandwich, took his money, and let him sit and eat in peace.

As I worked around the café, cleaning up stray dishes and wiping down tables, I found I couldn't help but overhear bits and pieces of Coach's conversation. I tried my best to ignore it, but every time I walked by, he was telling the person on the other end of the line something loudly enough that I couldn't help but hear it clearly and without any effort.

Coach had apparently been out of town recently and unexpectedly. Wherever he went, he sounded unhappy about how expensive it had been because he kept complaining about money he was never getting back. I sympathized with the sudden expense and wondered if he'd been able to make it to Joe's funeral. He was Joe's former coach, and I imagined he would have made it if he could.

He finally hung up and put the phone down on the table with a sigh. He rubbed his right hand anxiously.

"Everything all right there, Coach?" I asked from behind the counter as I made a fresh pitcher of tea. "You sounded a little stressed."

"You were listening?" he asked, sounding angry and alarmed at once.

I was momentarily flustered by the accusation, but I smiled politely. "I wasn't listening, no, but I could tell that you seemed upset."

"Oh, well, no, no, I'm fine," he insisted, still rubbing his hand.

"Is your hand okay?"

"Hmm? Oh, I, uh, punched a wall the other day."

I raised my eyebrows in surprise.

"When I found out about Joe," he added. "I just hate to see a waste of a young life like that."

"I definitely agree with you there."

"I need to go," Coach said, standing up quickly.

"Thanks for coming in!" I called to his back as he hurried out the door. His sudden exit seemed strange to me, and I wondered if my question about his phone call had offended him.

Over my years working at the café as I grew up, I'd learned that people were generally flattered when I showed I was paying attention to how they were carrying themselves. Whether people were happy or sad, my interest usually made them feel as though they weren't just anonymous customers. Every once in a while though, someone took it the wrong way, and I felt as though I was prying. Between his strained phone call, his hurt hand, and Joe's death, Coach Snyder seemed to have taken my question the wrong way. That bothered me, sure, but I wasn't going to spend a lot of time dwelling on it.

Business for the rest of the evening was steady but nothing I couldn't handle on my own. I served people drinks, moved them in and out, and straightened up in their wake. The time flew by, and I was pleasantly surprised when I looked up from the drink I was preparing to see Matt standing on the other side of the counter.

"Hey! What are you doing here?" I asked.

"Figured you'd want an escort home," he said. He glanced around the café. "I didn't expect it to still be this busy in here."

I looked up at the oversized wrought-iron clock on the wall and noted in surprise that it was closing time.

"I didn't even realize it was that late," I told him. "Could you go flip the sign on the door?"

I finished the drink I was working on as Matt walked back to the door and flipped it from Open to Closed. On his way back, I noted with gratitude that he picked up some dirty dishes to carry into the back.

"Thank you," I mouthed to him as we crossed paths, me on my way to deliver the final drink of the day to a customer, and him on his way to the back room with the dishes. Without my even asking, he stepped in to work right beside me, busing tables, wiping them down, and slowly making it clear to the remaining customers that it was closing time. I would never kick someone out, but I wasn't going to unnecessarily prolong my work day by not cleaning up until the last person was gone, either.

"So you work here now, huh?" I asked Matt as he joined me behind the counter after he had flipped the last of the unoccupied chairs up onto its table. I was fiddling with the espresso machine, making sure it was clean and ready for Sammy to use first thing in the morning.

"Eh, you know, gotta help where I can," he replied with a wink. He drummed his hands on the counter. "What else can I do?"

"Can you make sure the display is full with tiramisu? The fridge in the back has more if you need it."

Matt checked the display and then headed into the back room so he could restock. When he opened the refrigerator, he turned toward me, his eyes wide. "You've been holding out on me!"

I laughed and shrugged. "Monica keeps me well stocked." I saw the look in his eye and held my index finger up in warning. "Don't you even think about eating any of it, either."

Matt put a playful pout on his face but left the pieces of tiramisu in their containers.

We worked on like that, teasing each other on and off as Matt helped me get everything in order for the morning until the last customers finally trickled out. I locked the door and turned out the lights in the front of the café before heading to the back to take my place at the sink next to Matt so we could finish washing the dishes. We chatted amiably for a few minutes as he washed and I dried. I wanted to ask if he'd been to the gym and whether he'd found anything out, but I didn't want him to think I cared only about his investigative skills, so I let the conversation wander to Matt's trip and his work and funny stories from the past few days at the café before I finally brought it up.

"Did you get to talk to your boys today?" I asked.

Matt laughed. "Yes, I did get to talk to 'my boys.'"

"And?" I prompted.

"I don't know if it's all that helpful, but they did mention that one of the guys who's usually around disappeared for a few days right after Joe died. He didn't show back up until a couple days ago."

"Maybe he went on vacation?" I suggested. "It is the middle of the summer, after all."

"Well, I guess he's not really the type to just take off like that. He always makes sure everybody knows when he has something planned, like he's showing off or something. Plus, when he came back, he wouldn't talk about where he'd been. You know, the guys were just asking the way people do–'Hey, man, where you been?'–and he got all offended like they were asking him a really personal question—the color of his underwear or something. I don't know. Like I said, I don't know if it's anything useful, but it was the one thing they seemed focused on."

"So they didn't mention anything else?" I asked, feeling slightly deflated, as if my only remaining lead was about to go up in smoke.

"They did mention he was at the gym the night Joe died and that was unusual. At least, he wasn't usually up with the kickboxers. He was asking Joe about some money Joe owed him or something. It sounded like it was a lot. The guys won't come right out and say it, but it's pretty clear they think it's pretty suspicious."

"Huh," I said thoughtfully, wiping a cup with a cloth. "That might be something. Did they mention the guy's name?"

"Yeah." Matt laughed, passing me another cup. "Get this, it was Coach Snyder from high school. Remember him?"

Chapter Twenty-Four

The cup fell from my hands and shattered on the tile floor.

"Are you okay?" Matt asked.

I wanted to answer, but my mouth felt frozen by the chill that ran down my spine. Everything suddenly clicked into place—the money Joe had given Melissa just before he died, him having been attacked by someone he wouldn't have seen as a threat, the way Coach had reacted when Sammy mentioned Joe's death. He'd gone on an unexpected trip right after Joe died. I'd thought the cost of the trip had been what he was complaining about never getting back, but I realized the subject was the money Joe had owed him. It even explained why Coach had been rubbing his hand so much—it probably still hurt from his deadly fight with Joe.

"Franny, are you okay?" Matt asked, grabbing my shoulders and trying to catch my eye.

"Coach Snyder killed Joe."

"What? Franny, those guys are meatheads. I wouldn't take anything they say too seriously. I certainly wouldn't base a murder accusation on something they say."

"No, you don't understand," I said, finally making eye contact with him. "Coach Snyder was here. Today. And a couple of days ago. And he was really agitated both times. When Sammy mentioned Joe's murder to him, he had a physical reaction."

"That happens. Joe was on his team all through high school. He probably—"

"No, listen!" I interrupted. "He had a physical reaction and then he could barely get out a response. Today, he was on the phone when he came in, talking about how he'd had to go out of town unexpectedly and he was talking about *money*... that he'd never get back."

"Franny–"

"Joe gave Melissa two thousand dollars a couple of days before he died. Where do you think he got that money?"

"From Coach. But Franny, just because Joe gave some money to Melissa that he should have given to Coach, doesn't mean that Coach killed him."

"No, but his hand!" I explained to Matt about how Coach had been rubbing his hand as though he had hurt it, how he'd been so on edge during his phone call and angry when I asked him about it. I told him all about how Todd was absolutely confident that Joe wouldn't have seen the person who killed him as a threat. I went over every detail I had learned and observed over the last several days. By the end of it, even though I could tell he wasn't quite as certain as I was, Matt agreed with me that it seemed as though, more likely than not, Coach Snyder had killed Joe.

"We have to call Mike," I said.

"Franny, you remember what happened last time."

"Yes, but this time is different."

Matt looked at me skeptically, but I was absolutely sure it was time to tell Mike what we had found out. I had complete faith in his ability as a detective, but Matt and I had both uncovered information that we wouldn't have if we hadn't happened to be in the right places at the right times. Maybe he knew some of it—Melissa would surely have mentioned the money to him—but since Coach Snyder had been in my café only hours earlier acting nervous and angry, I was sure Mike didn't know everything.

Matt finally nodded. "Okay," he said simply, holding his hands up in surrender.

"We need to talk to him in person," I said.

"And you want to do it tonight?"

"Yes. I don't think it should wait."

Matt sighed. "Do you want to call, or do you want me to?" he asked.

I thought about it for a few seconds. Normally, I wouldn't have any issue making that kind of call, but given my recent history with Mike, I thought Matt might have been the better candidate to call him up and tell him we had important information about his case.

"You call," I said.

"All right." Matt pulled his phone out of his pocket and tapped on the screen to pull up Mike's number.

Realizing I needed to direct my nervous energy somewhere, I set about cleaning up the shattered porcelain on the floor. It would never be a functional cup again, but after being glued back together, it could join the legion of others adorning the shelves around the café.

Saving the broken dishes had been another of my grandmother's cost-saving decorating tips. She never worried too much about getting matching sets but simply bought whatever was available and recycled everything into the décor when it had completed its useful life. She thought it made customers feel better too, when they accidentally broke something, if they knew she still had a use for it. As I picked up the broken bits of ceramic and placed them carefully in a cardboard box, I kept one ear on Matt's conversation.

"Hey, Mike. How's it going?" he started. There was the expected pause as Mike answered him. "Nothing much. I'm just here at Antonia's with Franny, and we were talking about Joe Davis's murder... Uh-huh. Uh-huh. Uh-huh. Well, listen, you know, I was talking to some of the guys at the gym today... Yeah, Todd's Gym. And anyway, when I mentioned it to Franny, it reminded her of something she'd overheard in the café, and, well, after talking it over, we both think it's something you should hear. Uh-huh. Uh-huh. Thirty minutes? Okay, sure. Okay, see you then. Bye."

"Mike won't be here for half an hour?" I asked. I was antsy and wanted to tell him what I'd figured out right then, not in thirty minutes. I wondered whether it would be faster to meet him at his house or the police station. But I was also a little nervous about leaving the café. Whether it was logical or not, I was nervous that Coach Snyder might have thought I'd overheard enough of his phone call that he was lurking outside, waiting for me to leave so he could kill me too.

"Mike won't be to my house for half an hour," Matt corrected. "We're meeting him there."

"But what if Coach Snyder is waiting out there to kill me?" I asked, giving voice to my fear. I couldn't help but realize that it sounded even more ridiculous out loud than it had in my head.

Matt made every effort not to laugh, but he obviously wasn't too concerned about retired baseball coaches lurking in the shadows. "I think we'll be okay," he said. And then, with a grin: "I've been working out, remember?"

I laughed, and some of the worry lifted off my shoulders.

By the time we finished washing the abandoned dishes and locking up the café, we had to walk quickly to get to Matt's house so we wouldn't leave Mike waiting. That suited me just fine because my nervousness came back as soon as we stepped out into the night with only the streetlights keeping the darkness at bay. I tried to be subtle, but we had barely walked half a block when Matt noticed how I was turning my head to study every shadow, looking for Coach-shaped threats hidden in their depths. Matt reached out and took my hand in his, squeezing it gently and then not letting go. I have to admit, the warmth and strength of his hand did distract me from my fears.

We walked up to Matt's house just as Mike pulled into the driveway. I noticed that he was in his personal car instead of his patrol car, and I wondered if that meant he wasn't taking this revelation seriously. I hoped it was just that he was currently off duty and didn't want to be compelled to do any extraneous police work that would keep him from getting back home.

"Hey, guys," he called as he climbed out of his car. "I was going to apologize for taking so long putting the kids to bed, but it doesn't look like I held you all up any. You want to go inside and talk?"

He was already halfway to the front door by then. Matt and I hurried up the front walk after him.

Inside, Matt offered to make coffee, but Mike and I both declined—Mike on the basis of needing to get back home as soon as he could, and me on the basis of having tasted Matt's coffee before. I didn't tell him that was why, of course, but based on the look he gave me, I think he knew.

The three of us settled down in the living room, Matt and me on the couch and Mike in an armchair opposite us. It was an unsettling repeat of the last time the three of us had gathered in that room on the day Matt's dad died.

Mike pulled a small notebook out of his back pocket and flipped it open. "So, what've you two got for me today?" he asked.

Matt and I looked at each other as Mike looked between the two of us. Finally, I took a deep breath and launched into a detailed explanation of everything I'd learned about the circumstances of Joe's murder over the past several days. Mike nodded as he listened, jotting down notes along the way. He asked a few questions here and there, which gave me confidence that he at least felt as though my story was plausible. When I finished, I looked at him expectantly, waiting for him to congratulate me on a job well done. Instead, he leaned back in his chair and tapped his pen against his notebook.

"Well, Fran, you've brought me some interesting information. It's not enough to make an arrest, but it's enough to make me want to have a little chat with Coach Snyder. I'll go see him first thing tomorrow and see if we can't have a little chat." He glanced down at his notebook again, scanning his notes. "Is there anything else you want to add before I go?"

I thought over everything I'd told him and then shook my head, satisfied I'd said everything I'd wanted. "Nope, that's everything."

Mike scooted forward in his chair. "Well, then, I'll get out of here and go make sure the kids actually went to sleep and aren't driving Sandra up the wall." He stood up and shook our hands. He looked me in the eye as he held onto my hand. "Thank you, Fran. Seriously. This is good information."

"Thank you for coming out so late," I replied.

"A cop's job is never done," he said as he headed for the door.

I watched Matt walk him to the door, and I hoped the information I'd given him was enough.

Chapter Twenty-Five

Coach Snyder sang like a bird as soon as Mike brought him down to the police department. Mike was too much of a professional to say anything, but rumor had it that Coach even cried during the interview, and not just tearing up and sniffling—word was he was full-on sobbing almost as soon as Mike started asking questions. I almost felt bad for the guy. Almost. He had killed someone, after all.

The story turned out to be more or less what I had figured out. Coach placed a bet with Joe and won, but Joe had been feeling guilty about not paying child support, so instead of paying out as he was supposed to, he gave the money to Melissa. Coach went to the gym the night of Joe's death to try to talk to him and get his money back, but they got into a scuffle. Joe was younger, stronger, faster, and better trained than Coach, so in the heat of the moment, Coach picked up the first thing he could find on the ground that he could use as a weapon, one of the broken beer bottles the teenagers who hung out in the parking lot had left behind. Coach brandished it at Joe just as Joe lunged at Coach. The bottle punctured Joe's chest in the worst possible way and killed him. When Coach saw Joe crumple to the ground, he hurried to his car and left town for a few days, hoping the case would have died down by the time he got back. Little did he realize that skipping town would be one of the key pieces of information that led me to him.

Coach's arrest meant, of course, that Todd was completely off the hook. When he heard I had passed some of the critical information to Mike that led to the arrest, he came by the café to thank me personally for taking the time to investigate the case. He did not, I noticed, bring or send flowers. I took that as a sign that he understood I'd been serious when I told him I wasn't interested in a romantic relationship. I wouldn't have complained about more flowers, though.

In a lucky twist of fate, Joe had a life-insurance policy that gave Melissa enough money to get Emmy some pretty, frilly clothes like she wanted, with plenty left over to save for Emmy's future. The money didn't make up for the loss of Joe in Emmy's life, but it gave Melissa some peace of mind so she wouldn't spend every waking moment wondering how she was going to feed and clothe her daughter that month. It gave her the freedom to focus on being the best mother she could be.

Melissa thought about using some of the money to pick up and move somewhere Emmy wouldn't have to be known as a murder victim's daughter, but at least for the time, she decided to stay in Cape Bay where she and Emmy could be surrounded by friends and family who could keep Joe's memory alive for the little girl. I knew all of that partly because Sammy filled me in and partly because Melissa had started making it a point to stop by the café and say hello every few days. She and I would talk for a few minutes if I could. Making new friends and putting down new roots in my hometown felt good.

Melissa was in the café one day, talking to Sammy and showing her something on her phone, when Sammy called me over from where I was organizing supplies behind the counter.

"Hey, have you seen this?" she asked.

"Seen what?"

I walked over toward them, and she held out Melissa's phone. On the screen was a picture of a latte that, if I hadn't known any better, I would have sworn I'd made. It was a beach scene with a palm tree, something I was sure thousands of baristas were perfectly capable of making, but instead of looking as though it had been poured by some anonymous hand, it looked exactly like what I would pour if I went to the espresso machine and attempted to make the same design that very minute. When I looked more closely, the cup even looked like one of ours. I took the phone from her and scrolled down to see if it had a caption.

Beachy latte art from Antonia's Italian Café in Cape Bay, Massachusetts

"What is this?" I asked, looking up first at Sammy and then at Melissa.

"Scroll down," Sammy said.

I scrolled all the way down to the bottom of the article, resisting the urge to stop and read as I went. There, at the bottom of the page, just above the comments, was the smiling face of a man who looked very familiar. I couldn't quite place him until I read the biography next to his picture.

Jack McAllister is a born-and-bred Southern boy with a taste for travel and delicious food. He has an unnatural fondness for Hawaiian shirts.

I looked up at Sammy, my jaw hanging open.

"He's a food blogger," she said.

I looked back down at the phone and then up again at her.

"Don't worry. It's a good review. He only has excellent things to say about you and the café," Melissa said.

"He mentions me?" I asked. I scrolled up to the top of the article. There were several more pictures along the way that I hadn't noticed him taking, including an artistic one of Monica's tiramisu. Aside from his avowed love of Hawaiian shirts, I now understood the reasoning behind the stereotypical tourist garb—no one would ever be suspicious of someone dressed like that taking pictures of restaurants. Someone who looked like a journalist—whatever a journalist looked like—was more likely to draw attention. But a tourist? Tourists take pictures to remember every second of their vacations, especially in the age of social media.

"He talks about how you're really warm and friendly and how you delivered his drinks right to him and spent time talking to him. He talks a little bit about your grandparents, too," Sammy said.

"Wow," I murmured, reaching the top of the article and starting to read. I leaned against the counter. I had just finished the first paragraph when Sammy loudly cleared her throat. "What?" I asked, looking up. I looked back down and realized that the phone in my hand wasn't mine. "Can you send me the link to this?" I asked Melissa, handing her phone back.

"Sure," she replied. "But I don't think that's what Sammy was referring to." She nodded toward the door.

I turned to see a man approaching the counter with a large vase of lilies covering his face. I wasn't sure how he could even see. A smile spread across my face when he set them down and I saw that their bearer was Matt.

"Hi," I said shyly.

"Hi, yourself," he replied.

Ever since the night Matt had held my hand, walking home from the café, we'd been getting closer and closer. I was even now almost willing to call him—*dare I say it?*—my boyfriend, even though our conversations still skirted around the subject.

"You brought me flowers," I said, my love-struck brain incapable of saying anything beyond the obvious.

"Lilies," he said.

"My favorite."

"I know. Why do you think I brought them? Oh, and the florist assured me that these have no smell whatsoever, so they won't interfere with the smell of the coffee. I sniffed them myself, just to make extra sure."

I smiled, about to walk around the counter to give him a hug, when I noticed an envelope stuffed among the flowers.

"What's this?" I reached in to get it.

Matt shrugged innocently. "You have to open it to find out."

I gasped when I peeked inside. "Is this what I think it is?" Several weeks earlier, after his dad's death, Matt had sold his house and moved back into his childhood home—the one just down the street from my own. When he told me, he'd also announced his desire to use some of the money to take a dream trip to Italy before investing the rest. The best part was that he'd invited me along.

I slid the sheet of paper out of the envelope and unfolded it on the counter. Matt leaned across so he could see it too.

"It's our itinerary. I wanted to surprise you with the plane tickets, but you just print those online now, so it didn't seem as special. This way, you get to see everything that we're going to do."

I scanned down the list. We were due to leave in mid-October, after the tourist season ended. It would be a long stay—two weeks—but we'd get to see most of the country, from Venice and Verona in the north, down to Rome and Naples and even Sicily in the south. It really was a dream trip. I could barely contain my excitement. I ran around the counter and threw my arms around Matt. He slid his arms around my waist and lifted me up into the air for a second, as though we were in a movie. And when he set me back down, he leaned in and very gently kissed me on the lips.

Recipe 1: London Fog

Ingredients:
- Earl Grey tea bag
- Milk
- Vanilla extract
- Sugar

Brew a strong cup of Earl Grey tea. Strain the tea and combine it with steamed milk. Add a dash of vanilla and your desired amount of sugar (or sweetener).

Recipe 2: Tiramisu

9 servings

Ingredients:
- 6 egg yolks
- 1 1/4 cup mascarpone cheese
- 1/3/4 cup heavy whipping cream
- 1 cup sugar
- 2 seven-ounce packages Italian ladyfingers
- 1 cup cold espresso
- 1/2 cup coffee-flavored liqueur
- 1 tbsp. cocoa for dusting

Combine egg yolks and sugar in the top of a double boiler, over boiling water. Reduce heat to low. Cook for 10 minutes, stirring constantly. Remove from heat and whip yolks until thick and lemon colored.

Add mascarpone to whipped yolks. Beat until combined. In a separate bowl, whip cream to stiff peaks.

Gently fold the whipped cream in the mascarpone sabayon mixture and set aside.

Mix cold espresso with the coffee liqueur and dip the ladyfingers into the mixture just long enough to get them wet. Don't soak them. Arrange ladyfingers in the bottom of a 9-inch square baking dish.

Spoon half the mascarpone cream filling over the ladyfingers. Repeat the process with another layer of ladyfingers and cream.

Refrigerate 4 hours or overnight. Dust with cocoa before serving.

About the Author

Harper Lin is the USA TODAY bestselling author of *The Patisserie Mysteries*, *The Emma Wild Holiday Mysteries*, *The Wonder Cats Mysteries*, and *The Cape Bay Cafe Mysteries*.

When she's not reading or writing mysteries, she loves going to yoga classes, hiking, and hanging out with her family and friends.

www.HarperLin.com

Tea, Tiramisu, and Tough Guys

Made in the USA
Columbia, SC
16 July 2022

63566559R00188